The Killbug Eulogies

The
Killbug Eulogies

A Novel

WILL MADDEN

SQUARE STRAW PRESS

Nashville, TN

To Emily

CONTENTS

A NEW REGULATION

Captain Prescott,

Regrettable about the chaplain yesterday. Although I did not care for his politics, he was a man of faith and character. Given the state of this war against the killbugs, the Hominid Alliance can ill-afford the loss. As can we.

After taking your recommendations under advisement, I've determined none of these candidates would make a suitable replacement as spiritual custodian.

Nonetheless, since further casualties are inevitable, someone must be tapped to perform the ritual at moments of burial and bereavement.

I hereby order the following: funeral speeches for the fallen shall be undertaken by the soldier in closest proximity when the fatal trauma was incurred.

There is an old adage about how people dread public speaking more than death. For those who face what we face daily, this ought to be foolishness, but prolonged exposure to the inhuman conditions on Thisone Rock have taken a toll on morale, and the men have begun to neglect the welfare of themselves and others. Six months remain until the fleet returns to extract us, and if our number continues to erode at this rate, the result will be catastrophic.

Courage is nothing but what we find in fear of something worse. As commander of these men, I will resort to whatever means may increase our chance of enduring until rescue arrives. May this order make clear that not the least of us has permission to pass into that good night. Our salvation depends upon it.

Major Harvey Croop,
4,582nd Infantry
Interworld Hominid Army

THE DEATH OF OOGO BOOGO

DEARLY BELOVED, WE GATHER HERE today to inter . . . No. To dedicate to the earth . . . Look, Oogo is dead. Our comrade-in-arms, fierce and brave, full of vim and . . . I have no idea what vim is. Private first class, Oogo—Oogs! He died a long way from home, here on Thisone Rock, eviscerated in battle by a praying mantis the size of a Great Dane before our very eyes. Mine especially. That's why I've been chosen, me who was most besplattered . . .

Listen, a man as strong and true as Oogo needs no monument. Which is convenient, because in a few days the bugs will dig him up and hollow out his thorax into an egg sac. So, I won't flood your ears with empty praise. You all know the warrior Oogo was. Few men were as thirsty for bug blood. Most of you know how he became that man, growing up with us on Beta Rock, playing and roughhousing in the idyllic ragnarite mines of Beta's fourth moon. Always giving of himself for others.

You'll notice a good bit of him missing. Sorry there's not more of Oogo to bury. As the man closest to him, I should have put a bullet in the bug the moment it opened up Oogo's abdomen. But I froze! When the shock subsided, I might've fired the first round into Oogo just to make him stop screaming. I realize now it was me making that sound.

The point is, there's a hole in all of us now, no less raw and gaping—

Today we haven't just lost a comrade. A piece of our childhood was torn out too, yard by yard with Oogo's intestines. Well, perhaps I can say a few words to fill that hole, to restore for one brief moment the magnificence that was Oogo: full of determination, ambition, and courage. Vim. Yes, Oogo was all guts—even the bugs could sense that.

Mm, what else?

Oh! In the glory of his youth, he was a fantastic swimmer, even by Betan standards. Who could forget with what easy grace he parted the limpid waters of the subterranean pools above the ragnarite shafts? His wake etched the water's surface, the furrows gently shimmering with the carcinogenic glow of the ragnarite.

And first to enlist.

Let none of us forget why we're here on Thisone—what we fight for! Ten years ago when an interstellar hive of giant killbugs attacked the Earth, a cloud of impenetrable black smoke choked every living thing upon it. We, sons of ragnarite miners and exporters, took to arms to avenge Beta's most valuable trade partner. Our late comrade, Oogo, led the charge.

First to take his medical examination, first to salute his mama in uniform, first to board the reefer we shipped out on. First at everything, like there was something fucking wrong with him.

Since that unprovoked attack on the homeworld, the hive has mobilized no fewer that seven hundred fifty-one killbug species as combat troops against the Hominid Alliance. Of that number, our troops have encountered no fiercer opponent than the mantis, who with its double exoskeletal scythes simultaneously shatters a man above the neck and below the belt, stealing in one frightful instant both his identity and his legacy. When this particularly gruesome attack style was declared an obstacle to meeting our ever more stringent recruitment goals, the brass saw fit to deploy this task force, the Fist of Beta, to the darkest corner of the galaxy to destroy the factory where they are produced.

Well, to victory! Smear the bug!

Oogo was destined to become our most decorated soldier: for valor, for messiest frag, for most kills from a supine position, most kills with a melee weapon, most berserker rages, most cakes baked in a combat situation, most K-rations consumed without a bowel movement.

Most comrades rescued. This, my unworthy body, broke his longstanding tie with Gil Rasher.

We'll never forget what an overachiever Oogo was. You couldn't make a merit badge Oogo wouldn't push himself to earn. No matter how high you'd set the bar, he'd climb up and set out a picnic atop it.

Oogo was the first man I met at boot camp. Or the first to meet me.

"Achievement unlocked: first to greet PFC Timothy Archon," said Oogs.

How bizarre, I thought. "Hello" would do, I told him. My first impression: Oogo was a bit off.

Turns out, he had been in that special program for overachievers. I didn't understand at the time that this was a sort of rehab. For "chronic achievement-oriented behavior." On Beta Rock, billboards reported how achievement ruins thousands of young lives every year. But when I met Oogo, I didn't know him like the rest of you, I didn't understand I wasn't supposed to say, "Hey Oogs, race you to the top of the bio-refuse midden." Or, "Bet you can't eat more than twenty beastball kernels." I had no idea he would do that stuff compulsively.

But we're not here to talk about Oogo's addiction. We're here to remember the warrior he was, the fear he inspired in the enemy—if killbugs could feel fear, that is. Cheever tells us the Hive spent years investigating why sometimes when the ordnance starts, our men crap themselves. Their field observations could discern no combat function for it: our shit doesn't explode or ignite or spawn micro-soldiers like bug excrement will. So, they tortured human captives mercilessly for an explanation of what this "fear weapon" did. Monstrously resilient, our men spat back at them: "Nothing, you bugfuckers, nothing!"

Well, no one would deny Oogo was heroically *unequipped* with the fear weapon— unless it was fear of not achieving! Everyone here knows Oogo holds the Beta record for most ragnarite mined in an hour, under 18 division. We know 'cause he mumbled about it the way some people say their prayers, that weird litany of all his achievements he recited three times a day. He shattered both his hands in three places breaking that record. His fingers never worked right again; he had to get that special pillow just for jerking off.

But you only had to look at the guy to see he was built for mining ragnarite: low and wide, pigeon-toed so he could work from a squat. His eyes even glowed ragnarite blue. Everyone in his family had eyes like that, bright as the subterranean lakes where we splashed and frolicked during the flower of our youth. To my knowledge, Oogs still holds the Beta record for frolicking on a summer holiday, under 13 division.

This loss will be particularly difficult on his family. My heart goes out to the Boogos. I knew them by reputation only. Coming from an exporter background, I'm not as well acquainted with them as the rest of you.

Seriously, why aren't one of you giving this speech? Clarker was his best friend, why doesn't he come up here? I know he's not a man of many words, but—Yeah, I *could* give him a biscuit, would that help?

Oogo's father, Edward, felt great pride that his ancestors numbered among the earliest settlers on Beta. Equipped with no more than a laser cutter, they helped build the shelters where Beta's founders weathered the electrical storms until they finally retreated into the caves. Edward even claims the name of the rock is no less than the letter beta from the Boogo coat of arms.

(Although I have doubts. Sure, it's the same style as on the flag, but those pioneers were living in lean-tos made of un-mortared laser-hewn carbon blocks. Do you think they eked out a living in the freezing desert carting around an extensive font pack? Even the bathroom graffiti from those days is all Helvetica.)

At birth, Oogo was diagnosed with a genetic condition especially unlucky for a ragnarite miner. Because of his blue-green color blindness, he couldn't tell by sight valuable ragnarite from useless hermaphroditum, the two mixed together in the rock like chocolate fudge swirl. Oogo had to lick the stuff to tell 'em apart. We're told as children never to put 'maphro in our mouths, not only because it's more carcinogenic than ragnarite, but it tastes so foul some people pass out. Oogo spent his early childhood sucking a 'maphro piece just to work past the gagging. And let's not forget how that stuff ground his teeth down to nubs. The kid practically had to suck his meals through a straw.

Edward, whose blood ran ragnarite blue, initially refused to recognize a child with Oogo's disorder as his son. In fact, the name Oogo struck many people as vindictive. Edward always maintained Oogo was named for Victor Hugo, but at the time H's were rationed due to the Third Colonial War. On the birth notice boards, the H shapes made practical replacement parts in the chrono-cannon targeting systems. As a kid, I thought he meant people were too poor to say H.

Anyway, it's safe to say ever since an infant, Oogo had a lot to prove. "Look at that boy," Eddie would say, "licking stones like a cervopard."

Oogo developed an unsightly scarf rinse and spit routine so he didn't have to break stride with his sonic drill. The froth encrusted his mouth until there was no point trying to remove the stain. Girls said his blue-green smile was repulsive, unkissable unless brain-hammered—and the aftertaste in the morning, yech! But for those who knew him, that ungodly grimace was a badge of honor.

It's no secret that "First to Greet PFC Timothy Archon" is the only civilized exchange the two of us ever had. When training maneuvers began, Oogo felt certain actions taken by said PFC were ruining his squad's rankings on the leaderboard—and keeping the squad from unlocking achievements.

Of course, I didn't see the point of a leaderboard when

we were about to be shuttled across the galaxy to prevent some freak insects from copulating. We hadn't joined the army to rank, I told him, we joined to cockblock. Industrial dismantlement, the brass calls it. But you can't argue with someone with Oogo's disorder, especially when it's one the military has a hard-on for.

Ach-heads. You all remember the war ministry's strategy years ago, to engineer super-soldiers with an aggravated merit badge mentality. Crazies who'd do anything for a laurel. If—or when!—they became a liability, you didn't even have to kill or incarcerate them, just give them some psychotic repetitive task and they'd spend the rest of their lives running up the score.

But then the enemy figured out they could post their own achievement lists. Ach-heads don't give a damn whose they unlock so long as they keep hitting their firework fix. They will spend days cracking encryption codes just to get at the task lists. Their pathological need for validation—even from their own enemies!—made them invaluable tools for committing all sorts of treachery.

Gracious, look at Oogo, there's not much left. I'm sorry, I am so sorry. Here's the left-hand scythe of the mantis that got him. These left scythes aim for the face. The sudden pain of losing it gave the mantis such a shock, the right scythe missed high over its usual target and gutted him instead.

Claiming this trophy cost Oogs his life. "Most Left Scythes Collected Intact." If mantes didn't blow acid when you broke the exoskeleton, it wouldn't even be a ranking. I assumed I'd shot it off when I unloaded that magazine, but the field counter tallies it as Oogo's.

Meaning Oogs died with one more than me.

I only had so many due to input error: brain stems are auto-target number 32 on our rifles; left scythes are 23. Sometimes I got it backward. For months while Oogs was cutting a swath through the enemy, I had been creating an irate troop of entirely battle capable amputees. Shooting left scythes is useless since the right one is just as deadly and they always attack with both together. Most the of the time, I wasn't even slowing them down.

Oh, left scythes are 32, brain stems 23? Right, thanks. I'll get it straight someday.

Point is, I was leading Oogs in scythes by mistake.

But Oogo took it personally, told me I was trying to fuck with his rankings. I told him I cared no more about rankings now than I did in boot camp. He said no one ranked top in scythes unless they were going for rankings, and I was number one by dozens.

Incorrect, I said. I'm just a soldier doing a job.

"Let's check out your stats, Archon," he spat. "Left scythes, number one. Look at you, go-getter! Your other scores must be equally impressive. Right scythes, dead last; brain stems, dead last; dorsal respiratory fins, top third. Hey, seems like you can hit a target if you try! Jock shots. You're ranking pretty good in jock shots, you sick fuck."

My combat scores, he concluded, were a mess in everything except left scythes—yes, and jock shots—and that was spoiling. Didn't I realize he had a condition? At least his scores benefited the unit. *My* top score was just to get under his skin.

When I explained my difficulty with the auto-targeting numbers, he pulled out his knife and carved 32 directly onto the barrel of my boson demassifier.

Hmm? Oh, right, 23.

Well, it was no help at all. I kept reading it backward! On the next sloop run, my seventeen left scythes set a single-day record for the entire task force.

I needn't tell you, Oogs was fuming. At my bunk that night, he strung me up by the fingers of my left hand. "Do you find this funny, Archon?" he asked.

My arm was popping from its socket. Funny? No, I said, but I had an excuse. I suffer from what's called *numerical dyslexia.* In a family of exporters, it's as shameful as blue-green color blindness. I'm absolutely useless at managing accounts. Why the hell did he think I was in the infantry? All the sons of family friends have cushy jobs managing inventory in arms depots, but here I was crawling up shit sloops into the fuckhills, auto-firing at mantes while they try to cut my face and junk off. Couldn't he imagine the humiliation I felt, the pressure I faced to make good?

I gave every indication I was ready to have a good cry with him, but for some reason he got angrier.

"So, you're just slumming it here with the rag farmers, are you?"

He told me if I set my auto-target one more time to 23, he was gonna cut out my eyes and shove 'em back in the wrong sockets so I would read the numbers in the right fucking order for once.

I told him that was fair.

32, whatever.

Christ, I hated Oogs and his dirty blue-green grin. Where did he get off threatening me? I'd show him a condition!

Three times I painted a left scythe directly onto the back of my helmet, and three times Oogs shot it off. I got a couple nasty concussions, but the last one landed him in the brig, so it was totally worth it. When he got out, Oogs visited me in medical with a fistful of guano gardenias and apologized. He also said that next time he was switching to armor piercers.

See? That's the kind of man Oogs was. He always gave you fair warning.

Well, we started shooting scythes like it was our primary objective. Oogs was gaining on me, but slowly. He was a much better shot, but he also had forty-three other ranks he wanted to protect. I only cared about left scythes. So, while Oogs tried to keep our contest quiet, I advertised every score, both his and mine. I knew if you grunts knew what we were up to, you would try to spoil, and with the considerable lead I held, scarcity would work to my advantage.

It also had another effect: with so much fire now targeting a non-essential armament, many of the bugs had gnawed their left scythes off, knowing that facing a shortage of preset targets, our weapons frequently misfire.

To press this advantage, for the first time in months, the mantes mounted a counterassault. We watched them flood out of the fuckhills, wave after wave. The righty regiment we called 'em, for obvious reasons.

"Looks like someone got there first, Boogo," I said, smiling to show him what proper teeth looked like.

The auto-targeter prioritizes whole bugs before partials, so the few remaining left-scythed mantes exploded into pools of goo the moment the palisade guard started shooting. Oogs fell into a panic. Clarker practically had to knock him down to keep him from jumping in front of friendly fire to stop the bullets. Funniest thing I ever saw.

What I mean is, I was heartbroken by it. Addiction is an ugly thing.

Major Croop was furious afterward. If it had just been Hemlock or somebody jacking around, he might not have even noticed, but Oogo was worth half the task force himself. (No offense to Hemlock. Or the rest of you.) So Croop was going to disable the ach-counters altogether. Yikes! Oogs threw a hissy. Told us he'd sooner be shot than fight without them, and we believed him. Well, no commander wants to go to battle without his Achilles, so the major made an allowance for Oogo's illness and disabled only the left scythe tally. Oogs and I also received a severe reprimand.

But that put an end to nothing. There's not an ach-head alive who can't hack an infantry leaderboard. Oogs programmed it to continue the tally, but to post the score only to his glucose monitor.

That's when the scythe war really heated up.

God almighty, those were some fierce battles. The contest grew so ferocious between us, the killing got so hot, it seemed like this might become what drove us to victory, so long as we still had scythed mantes to fight. Oogs, of course, was death on two legs. My once-huge lead dwindled until he was about to overtake me.

But then yesterday, the moment of destiny came.

We had infiltrated the fuckhills as usual, up the shit sloops, to snipe the females during the act of copulation when their vulnerable dorsal respiratory fin is exposed. In the tunnels, we encountered more right-handers: blueys, ragnarite blue. As far as Oogo's auto-targeter could see, there wasn't an intact left scythe in the entire fuckhill, so it tried to recalibrate itself to brain stems as a precaution. Oogs was having none of that. He unscrewed the panel on his rifle and hardwired its computer to 32.

Right? See, I know.

Well, there he was, rifle in his off hand, firing rounds sporadically while defending himself with a laser dirk in the other. The targeter was desperately seeking, trying to locate bugs through the walls three hives down, firing in every direction. No one was safe.

Next thing, I hear a shout. Oogo had put Clarker on lookout to watch for lefties—loyal as a lab retriever, that one—and now one had appeared in the doorway! Its markings were another color: the poor bastard was in the wrong hive cluster, gotten lost somehow when it picked up the scent of the fight.

Hearing Clarker's cry, Oogs spots it. Aim. Fire! By now the auto-targeter is so overstressed, it explodes the barrel. Shit! Now he's bleeding from both the arm and the face.

But what a badass Oogs is, still fighting those bastards claw-to-claw. He's in such a frenzy, the froth and foam start pouring down his chin, picking up the blue-green grit permanently stained upon his mouth. I swear, he hadn't been in such a state since he broke the mining record back on Beta.

I know killbugs don't feel fear, but you could see their ranks parting around him. Normally, they push toward weaknesses in the line, but even fighting hand-to-hand, weakness was nowhere near Oogo.

What a gladiator! He puts his body between me and the newcomer, determined to not let me get a round off unless

I put it through him first. Well, he needn't have worried, I hadn't even seen the goddamn thing yet.

But Oogs wasn't watching his flank. Suddenly, he's ambushed, a half dozen mantes leaping out at him at once. He's pinned, bleeding profusely and outnumbered, a hair's breadth from death. Meanwhile, Lefty is working himself around my way, as if the bugs are conspiring to keep Oogo from the scythe record. The mantis sticks out like a sore thumb, his body hermaphroditum green against an ocean of ragnarite blue. I'm still unaware, but Oogs had seen him *through* me. Who's the colorblind one?

Behind me, I hear it screech its kill song.

As I turn to face him, the fighter is reared up, the left scythe poised above his head. I think, ha ha, sick luck, but fat good it does me if he cuts my face off with it first.

I had time for one shot. If I left scythed him, he would get me righty. If I brain stemmed him, he would acid bomb me. I reckoned myself a goner. Well, as much as I'd like to snub Oogs, I'd rather die with my junk on, so the hell with the record, I thought. I aimed for the kill.

"Don't you dare!"

All of a sudden Oogs came roaring out of nowhere, covered head to toe in bug gore. He couldn't reach the scythe from this approach, so he buried his laser dirk in the bug's thigh and it stuck in the plating. The mantis lurched up in agony, turning toward Oogo to do him a double.

Oogs' right hand was newly empty, the left barely more than a stump. So what did he do? He leapt at the bug *with his teeth!* What teeth? Those ground down nubs ruined by too many years of sucking 'maphro. The teeth cracked, but so did the exoskeleton, so did Oogs' jaw . . . and with a grotesque wrench and an inhuman moan, the scythe came off.

Of course, the mantis cut Oogs open. It couldn't have missed if it wanted. Nerve reflex.

With his last spasm of life, Oogs pulled the scythe from his mouth and slashed the bug with it across its own goddamned face. Then as the thing disemboweled him, Oogs spat in its eyes, giving it a last taste of ragnarite to remember him by. The fiercest thing I ever saw.

So here it is, the trophy that Private Boogo, Beta born, died for. Initially, I petitioned Major Croop to have it sent home to his family when the ships return. But on second thought, I'm going to keep this one—a memento of whatever these events have taught me. We'll send the Boogos another, one colored ragnarite blue, not hermaphroditum green. I don't know what it'll mean to them, but I think it's what Oogo would have wanted. I'll package it with my own testament of his unmatched valor, courage, and cunning. Vim. Fit to make any Betan family proud.

I'm afraid I made a bit of a mess of this eulogizing thing. Just like so many things, I can't take it back, but I'd like to close with a little religious sentiment, even though I'm not very spiritual. But neither was Oogo, so I'll do my best to use the words the late chaplain used. I don't know what many of them mean, but I guess they're enough to get a body buried.

As these final clumps of earth cover our comrade forever—at least until the depositors dig him up—let us not bury Oogo the warrior, whose martial prowess was unequalled, nor Oogo the mining hero, unmatched in hauls of ore, who destroyed both his body and mind toiling in the carcinogenic but achingly beautiful mine shafts of Beta's fourth moon. Let the man we bury go to his rest free of fuckhills, auto-targeters, and K-ration achievements. Instead, let us consign to the soil of Thisone Rock our friend, Oogo Boogo, who took joy in life, before it coldly unmade him with its cruel ritual of scarf, rinse, and spit.

Oogo Boogo, champion frolicker, under 13 division.

May eternal rest now be upon you, at least for the next few days. May perpetual life shine upon you. Wherever you are, may the gods of your fathers grant you rest. May your soul be borne aloft by waters as warmly glowing as the limpid ragnarite pools. May they embrace you with serene joy and peace, may you find the expanse of space a boundless pool for your spirit to frolic, free from toil and conflict.

May the tranquility of your commencing journey through the stars be the only achievement your soul craves. We ask this through sumthin sumpin. Ad saeculum saeculorum, Amen.

THE DEATH OF HOWARD GRAYSON

DEARLY BELOVED. NO, INCORRECT. Major Croop says I'm not marrying anyone. Friends and comrades-in-arms? All right.

I'm surprised to be asked back. Last time some of you complained I was less than flattering to Oogo. Fair enough. I guess you shouldn't speak ill of someone at his own funeral, even if he is a fucking psychopath.

Ever since the chaplain got his brains seeded by a three-story cockroach, we've had to make do with laymen's blessings. Sure, but pass the book along, I say. To Clarker, for instance. Didn't he go to seminary? Bible camp? Obedience school? I forget what religion is what. He might not be articulate, but there's none among you I'd rather hear speak. You guys are all squeamish about speaking. Bug gore stains you to the elbow. You gentlemen are the

Fear of Beta, your name makes the Core Hive tremble. How can you be afraid of talking? "If I go up there," you say, "I'm gonna be the guy on the slab." Fine. Well, I'm happy to speak on your behalf.

Ol' cad Grayson. I'm gonna miss that leering grin, Howie. Do we have that picture? I'm going to remember you just like that, leering for all your worth. Seriously, this the best photo we got? Yeah, I know he always made that face, but . . .

Mantis ate your head, Howie. All gone, yum. But decapitation is still dying like a soldier, like a man. Tallest in the task force—twice, he'd say. Rasher here contends otherwise, but let's give it to Grayson today.

Gentlemen, I grieve with you, but what a thrill to see one of us dish it out like Howie. What war turns a man into! Well, Cheever can give that lecture best. Cheever, why aren't you giving this speech? No one said you had to do it sober. Anyway, I never could've done like Grayson, but I'm glad someone did. A circuit of justice feels complete. Twice a day, every day, we crawl into the fuckhills on our hands and knees, up the shit sloops, to do what we've been called to do as Sons of Beta. Meanwhile, the mantis fighters grow strong and numerous in the hive, sharpening their scythes, left right, swipe swipe, waiting for us. To die the way we die, in filth—it ain't right. Howie was our revenge.

Unlike Boogo, Grayson I grew up with. Never debonair but nonetheless persuasive. Always said his first time was at eleven with an older cousin. His mother probably arranged the tryst herself. Patricia Grayson, what a viper! Just like all those Sandschu women. Mr. Grayson—Todd, was it? Patty's first husband—died years before Howie was born. Grayson was just her professional name, God knows who Howie's father was. Anyhow, Patty may have exploited men, but she appreciated them in her way. She *hated* women. Happy to wring any woman's heart out with her bare hands. Or, if she couldn't, to have her son do it for her. She tried to teach Howie the art of twisting the knife, but I don't think she ever succeeded in making him malicious. It only fostered in him an overdeveloped sense of kink.

Plus, who knows, a huge family, branches in every shaft-domestic, half of those Sandschus don't even know they are related. But some of 'em like to forget.

Those weird cousins taught him how to speak to a girl. Him being a kid, the girls thought him harmless. Whoops. Howie used to chase them around the shores of the underground lakes on Beta's fourth moon. Well, he was never a salve for the eyes, but he swam like a fish, parting the surface of the lake with ease. Let's face it, Howie parted everything with ease. If you don't believe me, just ask Clarker's mom.

Booyah! Hey, remember that scandal when the banister rail got stuck and Howie left her bottom exposed for six hours during the Guddling Day celebration? She was too afraid to scream lest the revelers see her. Howie came by about once an hour with some champagne. When they finished the bottle, Howie—

Okay, okay! We'll save that story for the after party.

So yes, Howard Grayson would fuck your girl right out from under you, but in every other respect, he was a decent fellow. Share and share alike, his rations or your cousin. If you didn't interfere with his exploits, he'd do anything for you. Back on Tirso Mavda, he picked four hundred seventy-two chromite slivers out of Cheever's ass after he sat on a cactus mine just because Cheever never made a fuss over that unfortunate affair with his sister. You know, that one involving the jar of pickled eggs and the crowbar?

If you can learn anything from Howie, it's that flesh is flesh, nothing sacred about it. He was a bastard sometimes, but always egalitarian. Women were women, men were men. The same went for the enemy, which is why he would scold me for how I jock-shot the mantes.

"Look what they do to us" I'd cry. "Have you forgotten what a right scythe is? The family thief? Don't tell me that ain't worse."

"Worse don't make what you do right," he said. "They may be the scum of the galaxy we're gonna scrape off our boot after we grind 'em into the earth, but they're people too, they just want what we want: good food and a bit of ass. The lady mantises may conflate the two, but those fighters are our brothers. Put 'em down the way a brother ought to go. A clean shot to the head. That's all I want when I die."

Six months out here in the dung pit of space, we've all grown a bit itchy. In time, we started circle jerking just not to do it alone. Grayson went batshit in eight days. By month two, sometimes I'd find him weeping at night, howling at that toxic shitheap the bugs have got glowing in orbit like a moon. I'd think, ha! that bastard, Howie, now he's finally got what he had coming to him. But I felt sorry for him eventually. Kinda.

Howie drew himself that big picture of a woman out on the rock face beyond the south palisade, just to have something to look at. Coney tits, hairy shins, fat thighs, ankles like tree trunks. He'd press his whole body against it, cheek to groin, but it only made him more frustrated than anything.

"What's the point?" he said. "It hasn't got the right stink. No use without the smell."

So, he tried to synthesize the odor. The chemistry of it cheered him up for a while at least. Plus, what's he gonna do instead, attend another of Anglewood's one man shows? (No offense, Anglewood.)

At night, he made little sorties into the dark with just an infra-torch and a basket of glass jars. Howie would get down on his hands and knees outside the palisade, huffing in the crud and the muck. What a nose on him. When the wind shifted, he'd bound off like a bloodhound. He came back near dawn hauling all sorts of foul smelling glop: thistlebeck, catseed, kingslaw, blattleaf. Then his mucks: kettlemuck, sneakermold, grindslime, peterdreck, and cola. Lastly, that weird gunk he could only harvest by moonlight. Howie had to really huff it good to make sure it was the gunk he was looking for.

If anyone got twenty feet from the little lab he set up near the dry midden, their eyes would start to bleed.

But Howie was never satisfied with the results. He must've changed the recipe four or five dozen times. Sure, it smelt like poon to me—plus it was non-toxic, sorta, so you could put it on your K-rations when you got tired of hot sauce. But Howie was a perfectionist. He said it all tasted phonier than artificial sweetener.

"Don't beat yourself up," I told him. "It doesn't taste half bad. After a few weeks, you barely remember the difference."

Grayson snorted. "Better used to that artificial stuff," he said, "because we can never go back. To girls, I mean. We can never be men for them again, the way they expect. Not that I care but . . . They warn the women."

"About us?" I asked.

He nodded. "I heard them discussing it on Starbase Tare. 'Look out for those boys on factory detail. A few months of that, they can't tell 'em apart anymore. Female is female. Species is irrelevant. Blue eyes, brown eyes, compound eyes, a broad's a broad to them. And they go for the kill.'"

"That's just talk, Howie."

He sucked his teeth and shot me that dirty leer.

"I can feel it happening already," he said. "Tell me you can't feel it too. Lucky for us, some girls don't believe the warnings. 'Do I have an exoskeleton?' they say. 'A red-blooded man can tell an apple from an orange.' Yeah, but he still might juice 'em both."

Then one day Howie woke up and all he could think about was mantis cloacae, or whatever they have. "Pardon me, punjab," he was ready to tell the mantis drones, "but I got next." I thought he was kidding, but he said it was just a question of feasibility, about finding a way to make her docile.

"But, Howie," I said, "she's a mantis; she's not even docile in her sleep."

He was undeterred. "A woman is a woman, Archon. Gifts are good, flattery is everything. Just keep her off balance and she'll tip."

"You're probably not her type," I said, "I doubt she'd find you attractive."

He leered, his tongue between his teeth. "She'd be the first if she did."

Mantes are what you'd call a tough sell. Even for bugs, they have beastly faces, and they'd never do *anything* you can interpret as flirting. Not like the fleetsheet bugs on Fulton. Those are friendly and eager to accommodate, with an almost cherubic complexion—popular with the merchant shipmen navigating the cluster. Some sailors report that, even with the rashes and pustules they get, they still prefer them to their own wives. Stock up on peroxide, I guess.

But mantes, on the other hand. Even out of the bath, they smell like death, and they're covered in thorny plate armor. So, it doesn't matter how still you stand: if either of you sneezes, she'll cut you into Salisbury steak. And unlike the cuti-cutters they herd up on Crowbend, female mantes never leave the fuckhills. So covet and jones all you like, there's plenty to keep you off mantis.

Well, one day Howie approached Cheever about his "wesearch." Cheever must've smelled what was up 'cause he denied having any of the data Howie wanted.

"Then what the hell are you doing in that hole of yours?" Howie asked.

Cheever said he was currently working on a topographical study.

Howie expressed his impatience as utter contempt for the jargon of military scientists, which ever since the brass had started embedding them with combat troops, has been replete with cutesy words like "wesearch."

"What about those camwas and wecawdas you've planted all over the fuckhills? What about those hours and hours of audio footage you sit up all night watching and wistening to? Aren't those translation algorithms you've been cwunching? Your computer drains so much power, we can't heat the bathwater. If you tell me you haven't begun compiling a mantis lexicon, I'll cut your fuddy tongue out."

Cheever smiled softly. He admitted the *wexicon* already consisted of several thousand terms, but he hadn't yet begun to document—

"Bullshit. Show me the transcripts," Grayson demanded.

Cheever, of course, insisted that the transcripts, like most of his wesearch, was *cwassified*, only those with clearance from the brass could read them. The security of the Alliance depended upon it.

"So how about you *lend* me a wecawda and a twanswaita," said Howie, "and I'll make my own damn transcripts. You're not the only one on Thisone with brains.'"

"I'm afwaid," said Cheever, maintaining his superior air, "the *wexicon* is the excwusive pwopady of Centwal Intewigence."

So, Howie bartered with him. He knew Cheever's supply of Chernoff rumka was running low, but during his muck-digging, Howie had discovered a root beyond the palisade that when fermented would taste not so different from his rumka. Howie would be willing to exchange this tidbit for an equipment rental.

(That, if you don't know, is when Cheever began distilling bwain damage.)

So, Howie videotaped the mantes in the fuckhills. At night, he'd run the audio through Cheever's man/killbug modulator, taking notes. Other times, he'd just watch the video with the sound off, the same footage over and over. When I asked him what he was up to, he said, "Working up the urge."

He also had long conversations at mess with Gilbert Rasher about the mantes. Rasher made little mantis models out of K-rations, and Howie would stick them with toothpicks. As Rasher moved the toothpicks to different spots on the model, they'd whisper at each other, Howie leering and Gil egging him on with his creepy grin.

Listen, I'm not a bug, and I don't know what bugs feel, but everything Gil did to the K-mantes looked extremely painful. There was lots of bending in ways mantes aren't made to bend. Rasher also mimed violent actions on his own body, unspeakable things I don't like to think about.

"Know your enemy," I overheard Howie say, "biblically if possible."

Finally, Howie went ahead and seduced them. What a

champ! Snuck out of barracks in the middle of the night and crawled up the sloops alone. Wined and dined them too: a salad of pestled drone heads mixed with sandgrass and mort root. On his belt, he wore a pack of tools he and Gil had fabricated in the forge: hammer, saw, clamps, screwy little pikes. Don't know what any of them were for, and I don't wanna. Gas mask, tranqs, some vicious looking drill for piercing exoskeleton. A laser dirk programmed to cut so deep and no further. A pair of hooks attached to bracer plating. Some kind of studded crotch funnel. Weirdest commando gear I ever saw.

By the look of Howie the next morning, I assumed the venture had failed. He was covered in lacerations, and he could only walk 'cause he was juiced on stims and held together by coagulant. On his face, searing physical agony.

"She was unimpressed," he winced. "Yawned through the whole thing. 'Do something exciting, human,' she said. Exciting? I'd stuck my dirk in her eye by way of greeting. It turns out mantises consider that foreplay—hardly even assertive! 'Like a child, how you mutilate me. I feel I am playing with my nephew. Are you larva or lover?' So, I put my gun to her head and threatened to take a dump down her throat. 'Are you trying to be adorable?' she said. 'What next? Are we gonna hide behind the corpse pile and tongue each other's bungholes like children?"'

Disappointed as he was, Howie made another go of it as soon as he healed up a bit. He was too invested to quit. But over time the failures started to crush his spirit. The mantis ladies seemed incapable of scandal. In their language, "bathroom" and "boudoir" are the same word. Same hole, same room! Most of the depraved acts in Howie's head were not only permissible, they were expected. To a mantis, a male is delinquent if he doesn't defecate in his girlfriend's mouth. That's how he thanks her for the privilege! A drone who doesn't offer is either inconsiderate or inept.

I tried to cheer Howie up. "So what," I said to him, "you're finally getting your jollies without degrading anyone. What's wrong with that?"

Howie crumpled me with his stare.

"The mantis from a few nights ago? I slaughtered her sister and lashed the corpse to her body while she slept. So, what'd she do? The next day she blabbed about it everywhere. That's inappropriate!"

"It's true," I commiserated. "Something like that ought to be special."

His face twisted in contempt. "Let me put it this way,

Archon. Certain acts don't mean anything if she giggles about them with her mother over breakfast the next morning."

I pictured Howie sneaking into the hive at night, at risk of getting torn to shreds by his lovers. But even though he had the wrong number of legs and all that deadly equipment, he hardly made an impression. Here he was, fucking death in the ear, yet he had felt less innocent as a child swimming along the sublunar shores of Beta's fourth moon, splashing the girls he fancied most. What on Thisone did it take to entice a mantis?

"Well, you made a good run of it, Howie," I told him. "I doubt any of us would have had the balls to do what you did. You proved something to us, so it wasn't a total waste."

This only annoyed him. "Do you think I'm giving up?" he asked. "We're gonna die here, Archon. We have weeks, months at most. We need something to make life exciting for the time we have left."

Howie was right, I suppose, we must do something. So why not the most insane thing imaginable?

Eventually, Major Croop caught Howie crawling back to camp before dawn. "We're not going to discuss where the hell you've been, private," he said, "but you're not headed to medical until you've made your morning run up the sloop. Do I make myself clear?"

Howie didn't complain. He just dosed himself with coagulants and off he went. He fought with a painful twitch not even the auto-targeter could compensate for, but he managed his quota somehow, just as he'd done every day before.

In the afternoons, between runs, you could find Howie stretched out on a stone slab, his knuckles scraping the ground, drool trickling down his chin. His half-open eyes would gaze out blankly toward the hive hill. Nearly dead from injury and exhaustion, he breathed by sheer force of will and enough chemical stimulant to kill a tanker bug. I doubt Major Croop was in the dark about what Howie was up to, but with all the threats to morale, he must have decided it was best to turn a blind eye.

At least until the juniors attacked.

Did you know you can cross-fertilize mantis eggs? Well, it's true. They have extremely adaptive DNA, a sophisticated re-sequencer that's activated as an emergency survival mechanism. You didn't know that because nobody ever got close enough to a mantis to find out.

Until one day on evening sloop, about four dozen hybrids flooded the tunnel. Two feet high, six legs. No scythes. Instead, adorable little handsies that came at you with a left-right smack smack. Nasty teeth though, and powerful legs that leapt for the jugular. If they didn't get distracted and try to rape your ear, we might've lost a few. Terrible fun blasting them, though, once we learned to grab 'em by the toes and play skeet with 'em.

The bawdy little leers weren't quite a paternity test, but we all figured it out.

"When they come at you," Howie told us, "you can shoot 'em. That's what they're for, just like what you and I are for. But no jock shots, Archon. I don't care if they are bugs, they're my boys, and if you touch 'em any way but right, I will haunt the fuck out of you."

Not sure what I would've done in the Major's place. On one hand, Howie had a responsibility to remain in fighting condition for the sloop runs, but his clandestine ops could potentially be more effective against mantis production capability than the rest of us put together. We smear the fighters by the score, but the females are elusive and built like tanks. If Howie was disabling or eliminating them in the hive on his lonesome, we might start making some headway.

Major Croop approached Private Grayson to make sure these were kill missions. "Don't care what you do, or how you do it—or God help me why you do it—but if you go, you gotta start bringing back some heads. You can't endanger the men for nothing."

Howie was distraught. Which struck me queer. Unlike Cheever or Anglewood, guilt had never wracked Howie about smearing a killbug. So, I spoke to him about it.

"Don't think twice," I said. "Those females don't treat the drones any better. One good turn, I say."

"It's in their name, Tim. Killbugs are for killing. There's almost nothing in that hive I'd have a conscience about smearing."

"Almost?"

He didn't reply for a long time. After all those maulings night after night, I assumed he'd just died, to be honest. But then:

"Her face," he said, "was hard, shiny, and mottled, like a bowling ball. Her body long, aerodynamic, and sleek. Like fucking a cave speeder."

"What?" I said.

Grayson leered at me, blood-tinged spittle oozing from his mouth. "Boys on Beta always prefer their speeders to their girls. They should move to Thisone and get themselves mantises."

"Let me call a medic," I said.

He told me about her.

Lost in the ancillary tunnels one night, Howie had turned a corner and come upon her waxing her exoskeleton in a nitrous pool. A delicate tendril of light penetrated the vomit-caked ceiling and illuminated her in its ethereal glow.

It was like a thunderclap, Howie claimed. At the sight of her, he had dropped his phosphometric ionizer in the water and received quite a shock. When she heard the fizzlepop, she turned and reared up magnificently, exposing her lateral endocrine nodes aglitter with beads of moisture. Stunned by her beauty, Howie nearly forgot to shoot. When he did, he blew part of her face off. When she beheld him next out of her ruined eyes, she began to coo at him, thinking he was one of the bibblepods mantes keep as pets. Then she tried to kill him, since mantes also hunt bibblepods for sport.

Through the crackle of the translator, Howie informed her he was a human soldier here to scramble her eggs with his seed. If her cloaca pleased him, he had a sack of pulped drone heads he'd grant her afterward. Otherwise, her guts were spackle grease. "Now part your dorsal fins and retract your anterior flaps," he said, "here comes the mustard."

She slashed him across the chest and told him to watch his fucking mouth.

Fortunately for Howie, in mantis society it's rude for a female to devour a male until he's impregnated her at least once. Nevertheless, Howie had killed the mood, so she insisted they spend a while in conversation before she could even feign receptivity again. With a hind leg, she skewered his hand to the ground and sat on his chest, so they could chat peaceably. Howie did his best not to black out from the searing agony in his hand, lest her weight crush him to death while he was unconscious.

He expressed confusion about her reaction. Having studied the mantis mating ritual meticulously, he believed he'd followed the protocols—to the hisspop! In fact, he even thought he had come off rather smooth.

But Howie discovered this was no ordinary mantis. She said she didn't think sex and violence ought to be mixed. Of course, she enjoyed both enormously, but the combination sullied them, she felt. She didn't want a lover to threaten her or swear at her or mutilate her; that's what her family was for.

Also, she felt lovers' gifts of excrement were blasé. "I mean, it's not like he did anything other than not starve to death." She thought a suitor should try to prove to her he could do something the other drones could not.

Finally, she believed in daily hygiene, which was why she was there washing in the nitrous pools alone. Her snobby sisters would refuse to bathe until after the next death orgy. If anyone found out what she was doing, she would face severe censure. In fact, just her willingness to speak to a male under a flag of truce constituted a social outrage. She was what her people called a filthy pervert.

"It's odd," Howie told me. "At first I felt nothing but contempt for her prim- and properness, for her slavish adherence to all the tedious conventions that make human life unbearable. But as I swallowed down one more howl of agony in that tunnel, I realized that unlike the human women I've detested, this mantis conformed to nothing at all. Her love of cleanliness and polite language did not earn her the good graces of her family or neighbors. Nor was she trying to impress me with her knowledge of the copulatory rituals of my species. In fact, it was me who was trying to do everything by the book in hers.

"If I was half the man I was pretending to be, I wouldn't have gone in there with a speech ready, lifted from a transcript written by some unwitting rival. As she crushed me under her bulk, I felt a gentle dignity in her absent from myself, and the shame I felt made me angry. Unable to tolerate it a moment longer, I powered up the cylco-cussive drill Rasher and I had constructed and got ready to jam it right into her lateral lymph stoma.

"But then I thought, why punish the girl for faults I was finding in myself? She was a naive creature, but elegant in her way. She still remembered fondly boyfriends she had eaten. The first time she devoured a boy's face, she'd been barely more than a nymph herself. It had made her feel all grown up, yet strangely sad. Afterward, she'd gone and wept in her mother's arms. Her mother scolded her for being sentimental over something as trivial as a man's face. But it had been so sweet, she protested, with its gentle drone nobility dutiful to the cycle of generations. That face had expressed fondness for her, as a woman, as an individual. It had made her feel something fill up like a balloon inside her.

"As a hatchling, she'd never heard such an experience could exist. If it did, nobuggy on Thisone talked about it. It must've been a dark secret, part of something people practiced clandestinely above ground, marred in shame and social outcastery. But she couldn't understand why something intimate as two people coming together to build soldiers for the Greater Death ought to result in nothing but a simple biological act and then lunch. This was heroic, was it not? The glory of the hive was built on moments like this, was it not? Then why should they behave as if they were stealing something from each other?

"You should have seen her, Tim. When she spoke next, she was on the verge of tears.

"'When I told my mother these things, she said it was me who did not understand. Birth and death are supposed to mix together, joy and war are one and the same. My outlook was a great perversity. If I had any sense, I'd keep these dreadful thoughts to myself.'

"Here the mantis hissed at me," Howie said.

"'But humans, I was told, were different. When I met you, I hoped here, at last, was someone who would understand me. But I guess it was too much to ask for.'

"She emitted a hideous series of clicks that echoed through the corridor. 'Well then,' she cried, 'I'll get off you. Have your way with me, and then I'll eat you right up. Praise the Queen, or whatever you people say when you fuck.'

"'Well, I didn't come here to get eaten,' I told her truthfully enough. I also said I found her physically alluring—equally true. That I hadn't come here to mutilate her—less true. That I was intrigued by her outlook on life and I wanted to hear more—more true than I realized."

Howie groaned loudly. "Cripe, Archon."

I watched as brutal spasms shook his body.

"Lying crucified in a dung heap can induce some rather extreme points of view. Pain gives perspective, you know? Anyways, I've made an appointment to meet her again after medical finishes with my hand. I haven't decided if I'll keep it or not. The appointment, not the hand."

When Howie had asked her name, she spoke a word the translator rendered as "Dungmeat, feminine diminutive." Howie tried to repeat this word with his own oral cavity, but she said it sounded more like "Middle Channel (for semi-solid intake or outtake)." Which was ridiculous, she said, giggling. She only had two channels for semi-solid intake/outtake, no middle one. Tee hee. But if he liked, he could cut her a third.

She didn't insist, but she kept teasing him until he'd at least shown her the knife.

"Still," Howie said, "I don't know if I want to go back. There are plenty other mantises in the hive, and none of them hung up on this shared-experience perversity. No, forget it, I won't see her again."

He looked up at me. His eyes were nearly caked shut with dried blood.

"But the name has a certain charm, though, doesn't it? Little Dungmeata."

When I laughed, Grayson lurched up and smacked me hard on the back of the neck. "Don't you dare snigger at her! Dungmeata is passionate and courageous! She knows how to appreciate her body and her lover's body . . . which is more than I could say about your Aunt Maura." Ouch.

Over the following weeks, Howie brought back the quota of female heads he'd promised the Major, plus a few extra. With fewer eggs being laid, the mantis fighters were finally starting to thin. If Howie stayed active, we might have had a chance of accomplishing our mission. Who'd have thought?

But the dreamy look in his eye was inauspicious. Anyone could tell Howie Grayson was suffering from more than injuries and lack of sleep. He was getting a little moon-eyed. On sloop runs, Major Croop assigned Pimply Kitt to keep a watch on him to see if there was anybuggy he might be trying to protect, with orders to smear her immediately. But Howie knew his feelings had become a liability to Dungmeata, so when the two met on the battlefield, he even dinged her a few times. And if she missed *him* on purpose, I couldn't tell.

Who knows, maybe they were flirting?

Well, what a thing! Howie enamored with a killbug. The biggest obscenity of all time! But sort of romantic?

Picture it: like some ill-fated mythic suitor, he crawls up the sloop in the dead of night. He arrives at her boudoir covered in excrement—alluring if you're a mantis. Mild chemical lighting illuminates the room. Anticipating her lover, Dungmeata has set the mood by burning a resin secreted from her own body. Howie doesn't dare tell her the smell gives him ferocious headaches. They embrace. The blow he directs to the back of her head stuns her. Her legs buckle, granting him access to mount. Her dorsal respiratory fin opens, exhaling a gas that serves both as sexual stimulant and hallucinogen. The effect is especially euphoric in humans, but Howie masks himself against it lest he shred himself on her epithoracic barbs in his ecstasy. They couple. Afterward, he offers her a dessert he has seasoned personally.

Then they talk.

About their hopes and dreams, about days of yore! Howie speaks of Beta Rock in terms a killbug can appreciate: where we pile the garbage, the reasons we kill each other, and how we dispose of the bodies. He also describes breastfeeding to her, in case she finds the lack of cannibalism among our species disturbing.

"Make me laugh," Dungmeata says. So, Howie recounts life in our shafts-domestic. Dungmeata finds the whole thing delightfully obscene. As does Howie. Nursing homes, for instance: hilarious.

"Queen mercy," she laughs, scandalized. "Why don't you just *eat* them?"

Howie laughs too. "I don't know! Isn't it absurd?"

Immediately each promises to devour the other the moment one becomes too sick or wounded to fight.

Then Howie explains about money.

Dungmeata's giddy clicks echo through the corridors. "If I want my neighbor's house, I just kill her, eat her children, and move in. Isn't that easier than working all my life collecting . . . what did you call them? Little Queen heads? Such silliness!"

"I know," says Howie, laughing. "Would you like to hear a poem, Dungmeata?"

"What is a poem?"

"Basically, a bunch of words. On Beta, women like men to speak poems to them. Shall I tell you one?"

"Yes, please," says Dungmeata into the translator.

So, Howie recites "The Charge of the Light Brigade."

"Oh, a poem is a children's story. Adorable! Are they all so adorable?"

"No, not all of them." He follows with a canto of Ezra Pound.

"Ah, I see. Some poems are the gurgles a larva makes while it's learning to speak!"

"Yes, exactly," says Howie.

"So, the men talk like infants to women, and this is how women choose which will make good fathers?"

"Apparently."

"I do not understand."

"Me neither!"

When the laughter dies down, Howie asks her, "Why do you eat your boyfriends, Dungmeata?"

"It's for the children," Dungmeata says. "This way, no repeats. Bad fathers don't keep contaminating the gene pool."

"Well, what about good fathers, who make good offspring?"

"If they are good offspring," she says, "I just mate with them!"

Howie laughs and laughs.

Dungmeata asks him to describe a sunrise. Too large to

leave the fuckhill, she has never seen one. The thought of the sun rising makes Howie nauseous, but he describes it to her anyway.

"You know how sometimes when you kill someone, they collapse in the water, and the fluid oozes out, diffusing across the surface? It is like that, like a corpse slowly leaking across the sky."

"Oh. I've seen that thousands of times. I guess there's no reason to go up there after all."

"No, not at all," says Howie.

"I can honestly say I've no desire to see the sun."

"Me neither," laughs Howie.

Then he asks her, "What's the most depraved thing anybuggy can do among your kind? Sexually. Name it and we'll do it, if it's possible."

She giggles. "Well. Exclusivity is just so perverse," she says. "It's the one thing I've never tried."

"Have you been with drones lately?" Howie asks.

Dungmeata nods. "Mhm. I ate two boyfriends this morning."

But although Little Dungmeata had other partners, it still angered Howie that the Major was forcing him to be disloyal to her. Toward the end, the female mantis heads he dragged back from the hive were particularly mashed up. I couldn't imagine what he put them through to get them in that condition. It was kind of touching, though. I never thought Howie might ever want to stop womanizing. But I guess once he stopped using women?

"You know," Howie told me recently at mess, "I used to think this war would be the end of me. Literally, of course, but I mean spiritually. I never expected to feel anything genuine again except hunger pangs and cock ache. But it wasn't until the war compelled me to murder every day that I learned what it meant to be human. I killed so much I forgot how to hate. That's when I began to feel again."

I looked at him with pity. "You're overexerted to a half centimeter from death. That is what you're feeling."

Howie sighed. "I used to feel like an animal. Even less: just a rind of skin. But now I see a point to it all. If it hadn't been for all those women, my mind never would have opened to the possibility of Dungmeata. It took me all those years, body by body, to get past the flesh. To reach the soul. To reach the point where I can see souls are real, luminous, and immortal. I had to experience the destruction of the Earth, I had to be shipped clear across the galaxy to a shit-wallow so remote it hasn't even got a proper name before I could I feel truly alive."

Here Howie leered at me, maybe because he found everything he just said hilarious, but perhaps all those years of philandering made it impossible for him to express joy any other way.

"There have been a lot of women, Archon. I won't say they all blur together, but they tend to fall into categories: shapes, sizes, ages . . . conditions. Whatever made my time with them unique was the only thing that interested me. Eventually, I felt I'd explored all the possibilities, all the permutations. I saw no reason to continue—me or the entire cosmos. When the war came, I welcomed it in a way, because nothing afterward could be the same. It would change people—physically, emotionally, from the inside out. Sexually is what I mean. A war this cataclysmic would create a new kind of woman again. The devouring mania I felt within me could glut itself a while longer.

"But then, Thisone. Trapped on this hell rock, our mission here a death sentence, I thought, why not? Mantis. Six months of this, they say a man can't tell them apart anymore, human woman, female killbug. Why fight it? Adventure again. What I didn't expect . . ."

Grayson fell quiet. I waited, grinding K-rations slowly with my teeth.

"I wasn't ready for how perfect she'd be. Physically

beautiful. Usually, I'm contemptuous of beauty. How boring it is! Beauty is often a lack of creativity in some respect. Refusal to outstrip even the most basic expectations. And yet I found Dungmeata beautiful, her scars and growths and calcifications. Also, her symmetries, the mathematical relationship between her lengths and girths. The touch and odor of her: exquisite, intoxicating. If I had encountered her as a younger man, I would've been repulsed by her, I would've thrown up. But after all these months on Thisone, I notice something sensual in her movement and scent. More than that, there's a vitality in her, something that sets her apart from others of her kind. I couldn't have felt this way about any other mantis, I'm responding to something unique in Dungmeata, something in her psyche, something in her physiognomy, in her and none other. It causes me to value her beyond measure. I am in love with Little Dungmeata."

He paused to weigh this sentence.

"And I believe I can only have loved Dungmeata. Of all the women on all the worlds of this galaxy, I believe there has always been only this one chance for love. But if it had not been for all the others, that swarming and confused horde, I never would have been open to it. I would never have seized this happiness. The long diseased course I've traveled, all that disappointment, anguish, and death, has been for this, this union, her and me, on Thisone Rock.

"Look, I know what you're thinking, Archon: everything I just said is the madness brought on by extreme duress. First, I doubt that, I do. Second, how can I care? I am in love. For the first and no doubt only time in my life, my whole being is at rest. I desire nothing but to be who and where I am. To deliberately poison that with doubt, what could be more insane?"

"Fucking a mantis?" I suggested.

"I want you to marry us," Grayson said to me.

I nearly choked on my K-rations. "I'm not a preacher," I sputtered, "or even an officer."

"I can't ask Major Croop," he said, "he'll have me shot. Archon, I know, everything involving you turns out a heinous mockery, but between that and nothing, I choose you. Dungmeata and I want to be an honest couple."

"Get Clarker. He's been to seminary."

Howie sighed. "Clarker is a good soul, but I don't think he's got it together to perform a ceremony. Listen, it's not complicated: just show up, say a prayer, and make up some vows for us. I would write them myself, but I haven't slept in three weeks, I doubt they'd be coherent."

"I don't know anything about weddings."

"You don't know anything about eulogies, but you spoke for thirty minutes at Boogo's funeral. It was an obscenity! Do that for us. Look, Archon, I'm asking you as a friend."

"You consider me a friend?"

"Fuck no. I'm just paying you a compliment so you'll do it. Look, I know Thisone is a hell rock on the border of charted space, but for once in my life, I'm going to do something the proper traditional way. I'm going to marry the woman I love, and I'm going to have a half-brained imbecile spout disrespectful things at the ceremony, just like every wedding I've ever attended. Now, are you in, or do I have to get Anglewood?"

So, I followed Howie into the fuckhills after curfew. I couldn't find a bible, so I dug through Anglewood's little stash of books and pulled out ancient earth novel called *A Prayer for Owen Meany*. It had a wedding dress on the cover, so I figured it would do.

It was difficult to come up with vows for a human-mantis couple. What could they possibly promise each other? They were supposed to kill each other in battle in the morning. So, I just wrote a list of questions and asked them to say "I do" afterward.

Do you reject Satan and all his empty promises?

Do you belong to the Communalist Party?

What's the French for goodbye?

Do you know the muffin man?

("Can't you ask a sort of proper one, Archon?")

Do you promise to shove and behold, cherish and polish, impugn and legislate, spy on and salivate so long as you both wear bibs?

Do you welcome children gladly, leading them into the killing fields as soon as they are strong enough to exert lethal force?

Do you have the time?

Do you believe this comb is a mustache?

With each I do, the pride swelled a little bigger in Howie, as if all the scattered pieces of himself were being swept back together. For one moment, he stood before me whole and healed. Even the dirty leer had transformed into something more human. It was as if a mystical presence had manifest itself in that little refuse tunnel and passed a favorable judgment upon Howard Grayson. "For this happiness, I have created you," it seemed to say, "in this moment I bless you. May the perfection of this hour journey with you and comfort you the rest of your life."

It seemed a pity it should end, but I ran out of things to

ask, so I said, "What splotch has coined, let no man investigate. Unpower the best in me, I now renounce you man and mantissa. You may kiss the bride."

Howie radiated joy. He stood up on his tiptoes, closed his eyes, and proffered his face. Dungmeata ate it in one gulp.

I scolded at her immediately. "You just promised to love each other as long as you both shall live."

She burped. "I did," she said.

"But you're pregnant," I cried. "Don't you want your children to have a father?"

"Don't be disgusting," she said. "I may be sicko, but that's no reason to bring the kids into it. Now, am I supposed to eat you next?"

"No! You weren't supposed to eat Howie either!"

"But you said . . ."

Turns out, Cheever's human-mantis wexicon had imperfections. Kiss? There's no mantis for "kiss," it approximated "eat." To be honest, she said, she thought this whole wedding bit was a devouring ceremony. Perverse as Dungmeata was, two people living out their lives together until one died a natural death made no sense to her.

When we discovered what had happened, she

apologized profusely for the misunderstanding and helped me drag Grayson's body back to the sloops so I could take him back for burial. She kept saying how embarrassed she was, she had ruined the whole ceremony—which had been quite lovely. The glow from the fusion tanks had been enchanting, the packing tarp we used on the walls had been an inspired choice—oh, and she'd never seen a refuse closet look so elegant. The guano gardenias seemed a little fresh but they smelled piquant.

(Well, the packing tarp *did* look nice. That was my idea!)

So today we dedicate Howie Grayson's remains to the earth. If he were still alive, we'd have to shoot him. Love is treason in this galaxy, apparently. But Major Croop sees no reason to make an example of Howie at his funeral since few of you can want to die like him. So here are a few words of praise:

Howie was a sick bastard. There was no recess so dark, so foul or pus-ridden that he wouldn't stick his thing in it. He called penicillin "breakfast." For him, gonorrhea was just another season. But in the end, I think he learned something about love and beauty, about the redeeming value of experience. God help me if I know what it is. But if such a thing as true love existed for Howie Grayson, it exists for the rest of us. If we ever get off this rock, maybe we'll recognize it before our factory-madness makes us stab her in the throat.

You know what? Forget love. Howie Grayson found *meaning* in this cataclysmic conflict. Good on him! In the day-to-day misery of our existence, Howie Grayson found a way to be thankful for being born. For Howie Grayson, there existed a moment, no matter how brief, that made it all worthwhile. Can any of us really ask for more than that? If you have not found your moment yet, keep in mind that it might still be ahead of you, even here on Thisone Rock. I believe that now, I truly do. Thank you, Howie, for resurrecting hope in me.

May eternal peace shine upon you. May your soul and the souls of the fitful departed be borne upon the wings of dawn, eternally in your house forever. We ask this ad saeculum saeculorum. Amen.

THE DEATH OF KITTREDGE HEMLOCK

GENTLEMEN, SHOCK OF BETA, I stand before you again with a heavy heart. Here lie the mortal remains of Kittredge Hemlock in one of the orange power insulators we use as beer mugs.

In the Solhendrik cluster, the native alcoholic beverage is called qolpa, which they drink from the yellow horn of the beast called the kashesh. Qolpa is almond flavored with a bitter aftertaste. It is green. The women of Solhendrik have one digit on each hand more than the men, four. Their pudenda are also green, slightly darker than qolpa.

Excuse me, I'm tearing up. No one could tell us the colors of stuff like Pimply Kitt. Yesterday he got himself impaled on our pet thorbeetle's heat rod. It cooked him from the inside out till he exploded in a shower of hamburger meat. Considering how gamy most of us have

61

gotten since we landed on Thisone, Hemlock smelled delicious. After seven months of K-rations, it was a pity not to make chili.

Kittredge Hemlock, not just a warrior and friend, but the little entertainment we had left out here on Thisone Rock. We've all traveled widely with the infantry, but Kitt was the only one to see the galaxy from outside a bug hill. While the rest of us were frolicking as teenagers in the mine shafts, each gently parting with his peerless skill the tranquil pools of Beta's fourth moon, Hemlock traveled the galaxy, beholding all its marvels, its myriad of impossible life.

Here on Thisone, we begged stories of Hemlock.

During the afternoons, we'd take shelter from the *pool-pah*—that rain of filth whose name means wrath of God. Driven inside the quonset hut we've built over the drop imprint, we'd hear the wet-dry splat-splash pounding the corrugated roof above us, and we'd press close to him, lifting our supplicant eyes and whispering:

"Tell us, Pimply Kitt. Tell us worlds: their men and marvels, seas, cities, sights unshared."

Hemlock told stories as if confessing sins, his voice hushed as he sat upon an ammo crate, fingers interlocked across his knee, one shoulder drawn back in a slight cringe as if anticipating a slap for the forbidden arcana he was about to reveal. The places he saw, the people whose minds he learned, distances traveled, dangers faced: we never cared about any of that stuff. But we listened politely, silent.

When he was done, we'd cry, "What color was the grass, Pimply Kitt? What color the sky, the water, the moon?"

He would reply, "Moon-colored, what difference does it make?"

"What about the women?" we pressed him. "Tell us the lady colors."

"Their skin was pink with a slightly bluish undertone."

"And what about . . . down there?"

Our single-minded obsession with vaginas drove Hemlock insane. With exasperation, he'd cry, "Orange! Mostly orange with black. What does it matter?"

But he would answer nothing until he dragged us through his confessional first. We had to let him unburden himself. When he was completely hollowed out, he was so relieved we weren't hurling censure at him—for what, I've no idea—he'd share all the colors in that wicked head of his.

If we ever listened to any of his stories, we'd know that small things upset him the most. One of my favorites—pay attention just this once!—was the story Hemlock told about the Asmet system. As soon as he arrived, he went straight to the coast and stood upon the shore. He spent three days lounging on the sand, vaguely aware of something unnerving about that place. It wasn't the mauve color of the sea, nor the sentient breakmoss scuttling up and down with the tide as it played intricate shell games in the surf. No, something else.

At night, Hemlock stayed up thinking about it, tossing and turning as the particle breath of a thousand-meter quartz leviathan blew in from the window. The next two mornings at dawn, he returned to the shore and made castles along the beach, sprawling complexes from which swarms of rake-toothed dragonfets waged war against one another. At noon, the tide washed the fortifications away, but before sunset, he'd build them back grander than before. Still, something gnawed at his mind. Three blue suns had risen, three gray suns had set before he realized: the sand was the wrong size. The granules were thirty percent larger on average than on every other rock in the galaxy. Fat sand had been driving him bonkers.

Once he spent a month on Cheutoi where the basis of architecture was fundamentally different. Every building leaned along the vector of axial rotation—to go upstairs was the same as going down the block. After only a few hours, he scarcely noticed the peculiarity of the scheme.

Mature males of the native hominid species grow scales on their faces instead of beards. The females nurse their young with a photosynthetic sap that collects in a pouch on the side of their heads. Through a system of periodic blood exchanges, she helps the infant during its first year to break down and dispose of waste, which without her assistance will accumulate to toxic levels. To Hemlock, none of this registered as odd.

But due to a geothermal quirk, evenings on Cheutoi grow warmer toward sunset instead of cooler. Only after midnight do temperatures start to drop. It wasn't the extra heat, but the fact that the gradient was different that rattled him. He always had a feeling the day was going backward, as if time was inside out.

Kitt's father, Lawrence "The Load" Hemlock, was a master miner who could pull exceptional tonnages consistently, not a psycho-burst rag farmer like Oogs. The extra ore brought in ample bonuses, but the bulk of his fortune came from teaching his technique in seminars on the weekend. When Kitt was born, Larry decided his son would live for something other than digging rocks.

"I can't remember the last time I saw the sun," he'd say, "since I felt the goddamn starlight."

Larry believed if Kitt cultivated a taste for finer things, he'd find life on Beta intolerable. He'd leave home and find a new life on another world. So, when Kittredge was old enough, Larry arranged for his son to tour the galaxy, to take in the sights, the people, the food, the music, the architecture, the creatures, the learning—the adventure!

But space travel was lonely for Hemlock. Not as affluent as other space tourists, but lacking the freedom afforded to vagabonds and stowaways, he bounced between the two groups, winning the acceptance of neither. Frustrated, he resigned himself to the company of things that couldn't reject him: temples, public arenas, markets, transportation systems. For him, palaces and slums were no more than three-dimensional models he could walk around inside. In time, he moved on to the countryside just beyond the urban sprawl, where most lethal dangers had either been quelled or else sufficiently documented so he was in no greater danger than on the sidewalks of alien cities.

Consider what this must have been like for Hemlock. Beta isn't exciting as far as organisms go. Everything stares blankly with the same milky eyes, and, after absorbing so much ragnarite resin, it glows the same blue in the darkness. But in the rest of the galaxy, where ferocious electrical storms haven't driven everything underground, life varies greatly from region to region across what the ancients called planets. The vast assortment awoke young Hemlock's imagination. He wanted to grab the wildlife he found with both hands, bury his face in it, flood his nostrils with the scent.

Since customs regulations prevented him from taking organisms with him, he decided to draw everything that flew or swam or crawled or sprawled, everything male and female, like a Noah's ark of naturalist drawings. He threw himself into this project as if no one had ever thought of it before. Hemlock had always been a good artist, and with the help of some drafting classes, he began assembling an impressive collection of animal and plant life across the stars.

"And the colors!" Hemlock would cry, "You wouldn't believe the variety of colors! Oh, the blues!" Hemlock identified three hundred eighty-seven naturally occurring shades of blue that were not ragnarite.

The universe, Hemlock said, is glorious multi-chrome. "There is a color for everything," he said. "Every thought, every emotion, every journey has its own hue, and I'm going to travel the galaxy, rock by rock, documenting them all. In black-and-white graphite drawings."

(Hemlock had no room in his baggage for paints.)

On arrival on each new world, he lost himself in his work as soon as his body stopped spasming from the local inoculations. But as much as he enjoyed discovery—expanding his knowledge, becoming a citizen of the cosmos—this was a very sad time for him. In the social centrifuge of the galaxy, he could almost feel himself forming his own stratum—not scientist, not artist, not traveler, but still possessing experience beyond the scope of most people. Even as he felt drawn irresistibly to this life, he developed nostalgia for Beta with its stark pervasive blue, its almost evangelical blue.

Kitt came to feel as if, instead of sending him on an adventure, his father had simply driven him out of the house. He spent most of the trip wishing he could go home, so he could speak with someone who understood the seasons where he grew up, people for whom he didn't have to reinvent himself.

But he hated Beta on his return. What a backwater, how uncultured! From one end of the galaxy to the other, he'd found no people more rude or less imaginative. The depth of his loathing surprised him. Having yearned for nothing but Beta's sublunar shores for three long years—an eternity for a boy—Kitt felt embarrassed of his home.

His father had long sheltered him from the mining life. Now it assaulted him everywhere: the dirty jokes and foul hygiene and the bodies that returned from the shafts each evening more mangled than the day before. He walked up and down his shaft-domestic gingerly, as if it hurt his feet to touch the ground. His shoulders clenched as if to keep the ragnarite dust from settling upon them. Whenever we greeted him with a slap on the cheek or invited him to let us blow darts at him, he recoiled from us. His eyes fixed on the blue stains under our nails, on the hunched back particular to ragnarite miners.

This is exactly what his father had wanted. Larry felt if the fortune he'd accumulated should have any value, it'd make Kittredge so disgusted with Beta, he'd leave and never return. Well, we all did our part to help. If he ever mentioned something he'd seen or experienced on another world, we'd look bored and wander off one by one.

So, if he became a prig, who can blame him? Beta hates anything with even a scent of the outer galaxy. Put a weapon in our hands, us Beta boys will wage war from one edge of the cosmos to the other. But during peacetime, we can't be bothered even to visit even the neighboring star systems.

Remember what we called him? Stamen sniffer? "Yeah, you like that fat pollen up your snout, ya buttercup huffer!" Or how we loaded a junk rocket with his underwear and launched it into orbit? "Hey, look it, Pimply Kitt's traveling past the moons again! Too good for this rock!"

Frankly, it was balls of us to ask about his travels after we got deployed on Thisone. It'd have served us right if he locked his lips and watched the shit splatter over the landscape in silence. If I was Hemlock, I would have told us to fuck off.

Especially since we scarcely paid him any attention while he spoke! All we ever cared about was what colors stuff was. Were the people blue, the sky red, the sea yellow? What color was the poop, the saliva, the girls' hoohoos? You ever get confused whether it was cunt juice or menstrual fluid?

Ten years in the infantry together, we still disparaged Hemlock for forgetting where he came from, for scoring no better than a double wavemash at the frolic. But everything he learned across the galaxy, all the knowledge that made him feel so criminal, was always at our disposal. Whenever we were getting overpowered, he always had suggestions for new ways to fight—tactics based on the hunting techniques he watched spearmen use to catch some sort of bear-lizard in the Freon cluster. But we only resented him for it. We told him to stuff his tater hole and play the All the Colors game. "Hemlock, tell us all the colors blood can come in. How about moons? Leaves? Snot?" He was always patient, even though we kept asking him the same ones.

"Semen again? Seriously?"

I dunno if you guys noticed this, but sometimes he just made colors up. Corsheen? Fake. Margarillo. Aberjon. None of these exist. I *know!* But I looked 'em up last night, while I was preparing these remarks. Mordishenta is some hinter-tongue for "Go sodomize the waterfowl."

(Yes, I do prepare! Why don't you lick a dinglenut?)

But if you ever paid him attention—well, listen because I'll tell you—he explained how over his travels, the star systems he visited infused him less with wonder and more just a sense of wrongness. The effect was almost imperceptible at first but over time it grew in urgency. Well, and not uniformly, either. It's hard to quantify a feeling, he said, but he estimated the incorrectness was proportional to his distance from Beta.

Our science operates on the principle that physics is

symmetrical throughout the universe, but Hemlock suspected this is only what we perceive while we stay put. As we travel, not only do time and space warp, but . . . It's something else, something without a name, which out of laziness we might call soul, but something we never suspected existed until we began to journey among the stars.

Hemlock conjectured we have a literal place in the universe. He described it as a natural vector along the contours of space-time, something gravity constructs. When we deviate, it twists. We don't notice the malformation created when we move across a world, like from one end of Beta to the other, or even from Beta to her ragnarite-rich fourth moon. But as we travel from star system to star system, the effect becomes more noticeable.

The nature of matter may be universal, but for some reason, *our* nature isn't. We are fixed—spiritually isn't the word because he meant materially—to a place in the cosmos. You, me, we all belong on Beta on account of being born there. Many of Beta's first settlers are said to have died of old age at fifty-five. Traditionally, this was blamed on aberrations in early warp travel, but Hemlock didn't believe that. Being in the wrong part of the galaxy for too long gradually chewed them apart.

And that grind is powerful here on Thisone, he said, here in the galaxy's remote corner. You may not be sensitive to moral anomalies in the fabric of existence because you slither up shit sloops twice daily in a perpetual murder cycle. But if they started throwing up some civilization here, that queer sickliness you feel today would still abide. It's not the deplorable conditions that create the sensation that the wind is always blowing at the wrong angle, that our digestive tracts are working, I dunno, sort of inside out. It's living on this rock, Hemlock would say. Just *being here* is an obscenity.

There's no *reason* for interstellar tourism, Hemlock would say. The truth is the galaxy, up close, when you put your fingers in it, is shockingly uniform. He cited the classic example: back on Earth when the possibility of space travel opened up, they began to create videoplays about galactic exploration. The stories often portrayed everyone in the universe as more or less human, or at least humanoids of a terrestrial variety: cats, lizards, slugs, whatever. When we started exploring the galaxy, though, we discovered what had been criticized then as lack of imagination was correct. These storytellers had intuited that life forms are similar everywhere. Geology too: the differences are functionally just a question of emphasis: hot-cold, wet-dry, verdant-barren.

For purposes of industry—tourism as much as raw material or manufacturing—these differences may be significant, but from the standpoint of documentation—and that's all you have if you're Pimply Kitt wandering across stars—you're just dealing with statistics. Numbers. The amount of rainfall, the percentage of potassium in the soil. So why was Kitt so intent on compiling this data? Because he was all alone in the vastness of the galaxy. He had nothing to do with himself if he stopped.

Hemlock decided to catalog all the flora and fauna here on Thisone too, including the insects, killbug and otherwise. Some of the tiny sort, as you know, are as dangerous as the Great Dane-sized interstellar kind, especially those bastard lithium ants with the necrotic bite. Pimply Kitt patiently made drawings of them in every stage of life, still wriggling at the end of skewers, never minding if a little sloop sludge dripped upon the page.

Remember that time Oogo shot down a skyrifer on morning patrol? Hemlock got Clarker to help him haul the carcass two and a half miles to camp so he could dissect it and make anatomical drawings. "Military research," he said. Everyone knew he was just feeding the monkey, even after he identified three new vulnerable points for the auto-targeter. No one could miss that frantic look in his eye, that ravenous euphoria. We almost didn't have the heart to remind him it was his turn to scrub the latrines.

"They are absolutely beautiful!" he exclaimed.

Grayson told Hemlock he was glad he thought so, because he was designing a rigging that'd net us a live one for conjugal use.

Hemlock was appalled. "A racehorse is beautiful, but you wouldn't wanna . . ."

Grayson just gave him a wink.

Anyways. Even when Kitt found time to immerse himself in his work, he still seemed despondent at the end of the day.

"Yesterday I spent hours going through my draft books, looking at the drawings, reading the names of the star systems where I found each life form, the latitude-longitude, environment, weather. Despite the care I've taken, there's no scientific value to this work at all. I might as well be collecting signatures of famous people. Still, I don't think I could stop if I tried, especially now. It's all I've got out here, and I think it'll be the death of me."

I assumed he meant *spiritually*, I never imagined he'd try to tame a thorbeetle. Those things have fission reactors in their abdomens! The west patrol once saw one mushroom just sharpening its mandible on a stone. How could anyone think of keeping it as a pet?

Hemlock estimated with a little ingenuity we could hook this one up to the generator and use it as a supplemental power source.

"Hemlock," I said, "you do realize it's irritable and it makes things explode just by touching them?"

"Relax, Archon. This is hardly the first organism I've studied that's tried to kill me."

"Well, at least wear a rubber suit!"

Suicide? Perhaps. But the look on his face suggested he wasn't expecting a heat rod in his liver. Despite the serrated edge latched into his innards, Hemlock kicked hard against Thorby's muzzle to get the sticker out of him, even if it meant shredding his intestines. Poor Hemlock lit up like a Christmas angel before he went nova.

I know, we never should have allowed it in the camp. But if it meant a chance for hot water again, who was going to stop him?

Then Joseph Clarker ate the ground meat, the dumbass. He thought we were having tacos.

Yeah, I know he hears, but look at him! Tongue lolling

out like he doesn't even understand me. Clarker, over here! Clarker! See? Nothing. That's Zen mastery for you.

Hemlock never understood we didn't give a shit about his philosophy. Big pictures, grand schemata? Come on, Pimply, just tell us what colors different stuff is and get on with it!

He'd complain we could just make it up for ourselves. The grass was purple, the sky was yellow, the milk was green, what difference did it make? We didn't need him to do that for us.

Still, too bad we didn't treat him better. We could have learned a lot from him. In addition to biology and zoology, he'd collected local folklore across the systems. The wisdom of worlds, some already destroyed by this war. But we never cared. All we wanted to hear about was vaginas.

On his journeys, he heard a story about a botanist who had scoured the galaxy for the most vaginal looking flower, and on Nyoduct Rock he found it. The coogilakka. In the local tongue, the name means cunt-on-a-stem. The first time you see it, it's a visceral reaction, it's just so carnal. Your astonishment becomes greater when you see the local women. The flowers are cultivated based on their resemblance to female genitalia. Meanwhile, a woman's desirability for marriage increases in proportion to her similarity to the flower. The two have been co-evolving this way for thousands of years. It's documented in the artwork and through a hundred generations of poon-flower poetry.

Hemlock said when he first heard this story it sounded revolutionary, as if it upended everything. But when he tried to articulate how, he came up empty. In fact, the more he thought about it, the more meaningless it became. Its only value was its ability to amuse strangers at parties, or poor bastards like us huddling under the shit shelter.

Well, if so, what's wrong with that? I loved the way Hemlock talked.

"I often speak badly of Grayson," he once said, "that oily-palmed man-slut, but I shouldn't: it's hypocritical. The philanderer and the naturalist are victims of the same disease. They practice the same pseudoscience, chasing the same vain hope, and ultimately arriving at the same lonely end."

Hemlock always said hilarious shit like that. I've no idea what it means, but it sounds brotherly and this is a eulogy. I'm trying to put him in a human light. And less a hamburger light. Maybe I've been eating K-rations for too long, but when Thorby cooked up Hemlock, it was the best thing I've smelt since I landed here. Yes, I know I said that already, but mmm, get a whiff! Do we really need to bury this?

"We have this vague hope," Hemlock told us, "that the galaxy, bright and vast as it is, will have something to tell us about ourselves. We believe clues to our identity are spread out among the stars. We feel if we seek them with a stockpile of chemical analysis sticks and a big enough clipboard, we will finally uncover all the secrets to ourselves we've been yearning to find since the beginning of history."

Hemlock told us it just wasn't there.

So? We didn't give a shit. Secrets to ourselves? Tell us the secret to getting through the day with our dicks attached. You know, something useful.

"Are the behavioral differences between hominid species environmental?" he'd ask. "Let's consult the data. On Walladu, hominids are herded like cattle, while the bovine race builds cities. Can anyone say what this teaches? Show of hands? Then how about this: one-fifth of galactic hominid species are vegetarian. Another twentieth is photosynthetic, but of that fraction, one-third are still carnivore! So, what does this teach us? Fuck all! Manipulate these numbers all day, it'll just throw you deeper into confusion about humanity's role in the universe. Did you know on a small handful of rocks, the cycle of genetic diversification is grinding down, and incestuous parentage is preferred? Everything we think we know, someplace in the galaxy is wrong."

So what did he keep doing it for? Why had he become addicted to this sort of information? Why did he keep forcing his sense of reality through that blender, one detail at a time?

"Nature is a false promise," he lamented. "She makes you believe if you dedicate yourself to penetrating her secrets, you will find the salve your sick soul requires. But it isn't true. Anyone who relies too much on nature for comfort and inspiration will eventually find themselves hollowed out and withered. Because she doesn't offer that kind of nourishment. You are just devouring yourself, that's all."

All right, that's enough sadness and frustration to bury any man. Hemlock, I don't know what prayer to offer up for you. The others, I wished their departing soul a safe spirit journey across the galaxy, but that might not be what you desire at all. I can hardly hope you find rest *here,* on this hell rock, with the *pool-pah* raining upon your grave.

Well, if I can believe you, your soul never left Beta, neither during the galactic survey of your youth, nor on your tours with the infantry. Then may that unmovable part of you remain unmoving on the fourth moon, at peace in orbit over the blasted desert of Beta's surface, watching as storm after storm leaves it unchanged. May you look down from that tidal-locked mining satellite, feeling at one with the stark beauty of Beta's monochrome wasteland. Distance, silence, uniformity. May these things not be a horror for you.

I remember when we were children, Kitt. We were playing upon the lunar shore and you found a finger in the sand. Many of us would have been frightened, but not you. You were fascinated. To you, it was a strange prize, a revelation. Only after you learned that nobody was missing a finger, that it belonged to nobody, did you begin to cry. Into your hands had fallen a riddle with no answer, and suddenly you were inconsolable.

I hope in death, you are finally free of fingers in the sand.

That is a weak blessing, I know it.

You were a stolid soldier, no one could fault you. You bore the burden of duty without complaint, you obeyed orders when obedience was called for, you assumed leadership when leadership was needed. Someday after this factory has been dismantled, when we have scraped the bug from this corner of the galaxy and—for God knows what reason—we decide to colonize this sector, your anatomical data on Thisone's native flora and fauna will prove invaluable. I guess.

In the old Earth stories, it's the devil who is truly omniscient, who knows every stone, every plant and animal, every microbe, every height and depth—and has a name for each. As strange as it sounds, this intimate knowledge of everything which God had created was considered evil. Perhaps you have discovered why.

If this was your sin, in the fullness of time may you be forgiven. That's the best I have. Pescium in patches, Kittredge Hemlock. Goodbye. Amen.

THE DEATH OF JOSEPH CLARKER

G ATHERED TOGETHER AGAIN. Of the causalities we've sustained on Thisone, this has been the most difficult to bear. Assigned an eleven-month mission completely cut off from the fleet, with no communication except those useless broadcasts that masquerade as counterintelligence, we knew that not all of us, if any of us, would see off this rock. Yet somehow, we never imagined losing Joseph Clarker.

Comrades, every day we work ourselves within a hair's breadth of death—twisted with labor, crippled with injury, wracked with mental anguish, ground down by fatigue. Every night, we lay ourselves in the regeneration units, having earned the peace of death with but another single day's exertion. We may ask ourselves, what power reanimates our artificially reconstituted bodies at dawn to face another day of inhospitable weather, indomitable foes, and horizons so bleak we wonder if God could have ever favored them with his gaze? The easy answer is, it's the gigajolt of electricity with which the rebooter fries our bones. Without this synapse-searing cardiac shock to restart ourselves, it's biologically impossible we could rise to face another dawn. Once we wake, our organism retains cohesion only with aid of the adrenaline rush needed to make the dash across the barracks floor to place our thumbprints on the console to cut the juice electrifying our spine.

How many times have you sworn when that sadistic rooster crows tomorrow, you were gonna roll over and lay there until the bed caught fire? Well, why haven't you?

Look around you. For seven months now, we have eked out an existence on a world human beings were never meant to inhabit. Every animal, every plant, every fungus is hostile to us. Every day, twice a day, three times on Christmas, we drag ourselves under sixty pounds of gear, up a spurting river of filth on our unaccomplishable mission to combat a near impervious adversary. Four more months of this before the ships return.

Some of you have a sweetheart back home. Some hold on to ambitions for the future. Some just refuse to get smeared until you get revenge against the bastards who stationed you here on Thisone Rock.

Clarker had faith. More than a just medallion around his neck, it was something that coursed through his body, nourishing his flesh, moving as he moved. His every action was its expression and fulfillment. He had faith where the rest of us couldn't. So we didn't have to.

Joseph Clarker talked about his beliefs all the time, I just never understood any of it. He kinda mumbled, you know? But whatever his convictions, they carried him into battle twice a day every day, up and down the shit sloops, no matter the weather.

My comrades-in-arms, you and I have fought in a lot of forsaken places, but nowhere has weather like this. Christ in a crate! Many rocks have both this heat and cold, the wet and dry, even the rapid shifts between, but this has got to be the only place in the galaxy where "shit" is a meteorological condition. Certainly, the only place where shit storms constitute an improvement in the forecast. "Aye lads, chin up, shit season be startin' again soon!" Cool in heat, warm in the cold, shit even moderates humidity. You gentlemen know as well as I there's nothing worse than a shit-free day. What strength makes you capable of looking forward to shit?

As I've said, Clarker had faith: unmovable, unshakable. Presuming it never changed.

On Beta, his strict but affectionate parents patiently inculcated him with . . . I don't know what church or temple the Clarkers belonged to, but they instructed Joe through short maxims, gestures, and rituals. They emphasized discipline, obedience, and submission to a higher power. His schooling suffered as result of this spiritual immersion—let's face it, he was a bit stupid. But whatever the faults of their methodology, this much was obvious: Joseph became someone who expected little, was grateful for much. From my earliest memories of him, tranquility suffused him. He accepted his circumstance no matter how grim. But most of all, he had joy in his heart.

I don't know exactly what sustained Clarker on this hell rock, but I cannot be alone when I say for the last seven months, Clarker sustained *me*. Who but he could look forward to day after day of this war? Even the great Oogo Boogo, who met each sun with lethal resolve, whose nerves grew raw with an itch only death-making could salve, even he did not enter the shit sloops each morning with Clarker's bounding eagerness. Yet while Oogo lived, the two were inseparable in combat, one acting as the eyes and ears of the other as they fought jaws-and-claws like a single entity.

And should Clarker, in his dimwitted haste, expose himself on the battlefield, he never had cause to fear, because Boogo would be there. And if not him, someone else would pluck him from harm, not just out of loyalty to Clarker, but as if their own lives depended on it. Because Clarker was this task force's good luck charm, our sacred totem, the only excuse for our continued survival.

Count the men you see gathered here today. They make up the entire human presence on Thisone, minus the palisade guard and Cheever, who's . . . I'm told he's sick. Compare that number against the insect population, which we estimate at eight billion on this peninsula alone. Our cover of secrecy was blown months ago. The bugs should have long since eradicated us. So why are we still alive? Why have they not swarmed our camp and exterminated us? I believed, as did you, that it was Clarker who preserved us by virtue of his divine favor—or disgusting luck, whatever you wanted to call it. We imagined that whatever otherworldly power granted its favor to Clarker—and, by extension, us—might hold sway over the killbugs as well. But now Clarker's gone, and we're still here. Any explanations?

Clarker's grace remains with us, stained indelibly upon our skin. After the dragon-wasp tore off his arms, and the cater-roarer clamped Joe's lower half in its jaws, it began flailing about, waving Clarker's mutilated body around like a censer. The hot blood spurted from his body and splashed upon our faces. Perhaps in these last moments, with his dying heartbeats, he imparted that divine succor upon us. (Something funny, Gil?) In any case, I have no doubt the blessing Clarker bestowed upon us will protect us. Until we die.

Clarker was always our good luck charm, even back on Beta. When picking teams for the frolic, Clarker was always last. "And Clarker for luck," the team captain would say. I'm not sure Clarker had another use. He damn sure didn't understand the rules. He wore a team pinny, but usually he forgot what side he was on. But it was still an advantage to have him. Clarker's team, forced to play "shorthanded," would frolic twice as hard. Meanwhile, the other side had to worry about getting too close to him, since his aggressive splashing was more dangerous than skillful.

Before the match, his teammates would rub that holy symbol around his neck for luck. What shape was it again? Circle? Pentagon? Cloud? Anyway, they'd all rub it, and Clarker would mumble something. Bless you, I suppose?

Might have been cursing them out for all you could tell. Did Clarker even know how to talk? I dunno.

But let's not forget what a wonderful swimmer Clarker was. Nobody paddled across the surface of a sublunar lake like Clarker. How come he never won any awards for that? He really had no peers, it was like he was built for the water. It slid off his body like duck-sass, whatever that is.

But the worst miner ever. The best you could do was to keep him from hurting himself.

He'd go at it with enthusiasm, though, sweating profusely, pulverizing that valuable rag ore with the drill bit. In a few minutes, there'd be nothing left but a worthless, lung-killing cloud. Oh, how we cheered him on!

"Who the sam-hain gave Clarker a drill," the foreman would cry. "Is this someone's idea of a joke?" He was furious: whoever drilled that vein afterward would have a bitch of a time not reducing the rest of the ore to shattered fragments. Once it cost us the better part of the summer working off the damage Clarker caused in half an hour. But which of us complained? Who regretted it for a moment? No one. It was always "Go, Joe, go!" Now, if I had done that, or Waldorf or Anglewood, that poor bastard would've been disappeared under an elevator shaft. Clarker, it made a hero.

Only his family never held him in high esteem. Because he was wild and rambunctious, sometimes when they went out, they kept him on a tether. If we asked nicely, they might let him off, but otherwise he just tried to pretend he didn't notice.

Do you know what I once heard his parents say? "Our only regret in life is that we never had a son." You laugh, but I was heartbroken to hear it. Just because he spoke poorly and ate like a slob and farted without embarrassment. Hey, the Clarkers acknowledge their three daughters. They're not much prettier—and have no better manners! You find that funny too, but gentlemen, think about Joe, we bury him today for Christ's sake. And remember how they addressed him: "Here, stupid. This way, stupid. Hey stupid, eat up." Imagine if Francis of Assisi was treated the same way! Because for my money, Clarker was no less holy, Francis no more bright, and neither more beloved by those who knew them. Only the families turned their backs. The Clarkers and the Of Assisis.

Joseph didn't go to school with us, which was another disservice the Clarkers paid him. They sent him downworld for special education. More religious training, I suppose. Again, I don't know the denomination, but Clarker was no damn fun after that. Before, he'd been a carefree, kinetic chaos. Now, he just sat there with a stern look on his face for more than an hour at a time. I'd never understood much of what Joe had said previously, but afterward he seldom spoke at all, even when you addressed him directly. The Clarkers felt all this spirituality made him easier to manage, but they'd killed off the better part of him, that quintessentially Betan attitude towards life: grab whatever's good with your teeth and shake it for all it's worth.

Nevertheless, I can't deny a quiet nobility had been instilled in him. His eyes were as stupid as ever, but they now possessed confidence, an inner strength. Between that and a fifth-grade education, I'd rather have the schooling, but I was forced to admit it gave Joe dignity. Gravitas.

Which mattered. We would not have endangered ourselves to protect Clarker if he were merely a medallion-wearer and a mutterer of incomprehensibles. He had a quality that made him dear to us. Smearing bug scum may make you righteous, but nobody except Clarker could kill all day and remain innocent. Only I hate to call it innocence, an insult for a warrior, brave and fierce. He was mostly useless with a rifle, but terrifying hand-to-hand. No wonder indomitable Boogo kept him close. Other than Boogo, Clarker's the only one I've seen kill a mantis with his teeth. But he was a killer with soul, and purity infused him even under duress.

Remember the time Major Croop asked him to guard the south palisade and then forgot about him? Clarker stood two and a half days out in the rain, heat, and shit without sleep, barely blinking. Or the time Cheever got drunk and accidentally incinerated half the week's rations, so we all had to tighten our belts? Clarker hardly made a whimper, just ate his own shit, ate everybody's shit. If anyone else had degraded himself that way, he'd still be hearing about it, even at his own funeral. But with Clarker, it's just something we understood he did for the good of the task force. Bless him!

Where did that charisma come from, the shit-eating likeability? He wasn't good looking, none of you would say that, yet everyone always took to him. Back on Beta, he was very popular with the girls, they always ran up to greet him, showering him with chaste kisses before letting him sleep with his head in their laps.

One day, while I was out on patrol, Clarker snuck into the barracks and destroyed my bunk. I'll never know why. He upturned everything, shredded the bedding, dragged my whole kit out into the filth. I decided to kill him, then and there. But beholding his sad eyes, hearing his incomprehensible whimper of apology, my anger simply burst. It's unmanly to admit this, but instead of cutting his throat, I embraced him like a brother. I buried my nose into his body and breathed in his damp stink. I practically begged forgiveness from *him*!

That's the power he had, that's how good a man Clarker was. In fact, it's hard for me to think the name "Clarker" without the word "good" springing at its heels. "Good Clarker, gooood!" I can't help it! When I think back on all the people I've known—saints and bastards both—that murdering shit-eater always stands out the most warmly.

Because Clarker loved his comrades-in-arms. In this whole deployment, he was the only one to harbor genuine affection for the others. Yes, Clarker loved us! And he took Oogo's death particularly badly. Clarker loved to fight, mostly because Oogo fought and Clarker loved to be with Oogo. They sustained each other, Clarker the only light of humanity Oogo could see through that cloud of ach-headedness. Out of loyalty, Clarker would've torn the throat out of anyone Oogo told him to—a craghopper or one of us—and done it with childlike joy at pleasing Oogo. When Oogo died, Clarker whimpered for days, almost forgetting who and where he was, like he didn't want to kill anymore, like it was no longer worth it.

I tried to talk Clarker out of his funk. He lay like a mass upon the ground, up to his eyeballs in bugshit, depressed or just keeping cool, I don't know. In case he was listening to me, I said that for a warrior like Oogo, there was no good way to die except in combat, in one last ferocious act that demonstrated the indomitability of his spirit. Yes, Oogo's death had come sooner than we may have hoped, but as his friends, ultimately, we could have wished no other end for him. To love a thing, I explained to his stupid face, means to yearn, in one way or another, that one day it will be the death of you. Well, Oogo certainly loved to fight. And wherever Oogo's spirit was now, it was satisfied. I asked Clarker if he understood.

Clarker looked up at me with those puppy dog eyes. Sadness, love, and acceptance shown from him so warmly, I instantly felt like the fool advising the sage. We embraced, my body pressed hard against his, a little shit sloppy, grant you, but afterward Clarker fought at my side, not with the same joy and ferocity as next to Oogo, but with a profound empathy which someone as superficial as I cannot hope to fathom.

A week or two before Oogo got smeared, the great warrior and I were up on Cavendale Ridge, looking out over all of you. "Each one of them," he said, "possesses a soul that has cracked under the weight of this endless, pointless mission. All except you and Clarker. Clarker's soul is just fine. And you, Archon, you never had a soul to break."

While I was preparing my remarks for today, I thought about this and what it meant. What did Clarker possess that Oogo felt was broken in you and absent in me?

Hemlock was always wary of him. Thisone Rock is rife with all sorts of deadly and disgusting surprises, but only Clarker made him uneasy. Hemlock even held his breath around him.

When I suggested that what he felt from Clarker was his aura as a holy man, Hemlock said:

"I don't think it's right to call Clarker a man, Archon."

"Well, if he's not a man," I asked, "what is he?"

"He's a hellbeast."

Hemlock shunned Clarker in the barracks and avoided fighting anywhere near him if he could. This deep dislike had persisted from the early days of the war.

After Earth had been destroyed, you, my brethren, the Comeuppance of Beta, filled the recruitment offices, offering your bodies and your valor to the front lines. Our late comrade was among you.

"Joseph too!" everyone cried, "Joseph Clarker is also

going to war!" Well, why wouldn't he? Should anyone be astonished? That someone who had parted the ragnarite pools of the fourth moon should now bare his forearms and vow to shed blood with us, is that cause for surprise?

The odd thing was that he didn't attend boot camp with us. Once again, Clarker was singled out for special training. Another absence, an even stranger transformation. When he returned, his posture had become somehow straighter, his jaw stronger, his eyes more deeply set. Yet the overall impact struck us as perverse. What can I say? If the first time he was sent away he was touched by God, now he stood defiled by him. Returned to the limpid pools of Beta's fourth moon, the shadow he cast by the carcinogenic glow of the ragnarite seemed to fill even Clarker with fear. "Sweet mercy," I gasped, "what have they done to you?"

"We'll make a man out of him!" That's what the directors of that weird military program had promised. Well, what was he before, I ask?

Hush, all of you.

Listen, I know this war is the worst thing to ever happen. But when I see the early pictures of us in uniform, I feel that grand ol' nostalgia: "Has the galaxy fallen so far,"

I chuckle, "that it's ready to turn to us? Well, bring it: These bastards here will be ready."

The first time I saw Clarker in boots, I shuddered. The way you try to shake off a nightmare.

That Clarker was born to kill, I can't deny—yet it was an obscenity to make him war. Clarker with a drill on the fourth moon, what joy to watch! But Clarker with a rifle in his fists—did he always have fists?—was simply too much to bear. When they conscripted him, I felt humanity had already lost.

The military declared Joe's combat training a "failure," but he nevertheless "met minimal combat proficiency," so they sent him to the line where they could forget their mistakes. Well, we were happy to have him. "Unsuccessful in significantly augmenting core intelligence." So what? Since when is being a soldier about smarts? "Cannot execute complex commands with any precision." Sure, he'll be at home with the Beta boys, send him to us. "Dietary habits deplorable." Do you think anyone here eats grains of rice one at a time with chopsticks? Besides, one more Beta dead is one more Beta proud. The galaxy will remember the price we paid here. Even our dogs died fighting for you!

I've told you I hardly understood a word Clarker said.

But he had a holy, oracular voice that erupted from his entire body. Bigger than language, more than words, it was *noise*.

Remember when the chaplain was still alive, before larvae started crawling out of his face during morning prayers, do you remember what he said to us? Anything, I mean? I can still see him still huddled over his little book, the ribbon on his shoulder that meant sorta-holy-guy. I remember the high solemn face, the fleshy but firm lips, the slightly hawkish nose. I remember how he closed his eyes before he spoke, like even about biscuits or something, as if his words were born in the pit of his stomach and flung high toward heaven—but always measured to a sixteenth of an inch, as if he dared to speak no word unfit for God's ear. I see it like it was yesterday. But it's a silent film. It's as if God—or man seeking solace in God—has nothing to say. And nobody among us was more intelligent or more articulate than the chaplain.

But when *Clarker* spoke, in his almost unforgivable simplicity, by God he made *noise*. He tore down heaven or he raised hell, and the great invisible mysteries were *with us* as he spoke. The terror, the power—inscrutable, intangible, immovable—issued raw from his throat, in roars and pops that clung to the nooks and crannies of the limitless. The sound gave shape to that unseen power, unreachable by vows and unbendable by entreaty, which guides our fate.

Whenever an aboveground skirmish was about to begin, Clarker would stand upon a high point. Over the scurry and chatter of the advancing enemy, the outcome of that battle would emerge with prescience from his throat: every ordnance fired, every wound received, every life brought to term. Like the opening to a great epic, it foretold the victories and agonies to come. It gave us both the courage to face death and the strength to keep fighting when death may have seemed easier.

So, let me invite you. One last time, see Clarker upon the hill. The archangels themselves could not have inspired more dread piercing the air above on wing, the shadow of their lances advancing over the earth, their faces shining with the light of wisdom and infinite love. Death-dealing, buoyed-in-the-air love! Clarker was our demon of love: the holy terrors followed him, over the fuckhills and down the shitvalleys, the Judgment of Beta, resisting then crushing the indomitable alien enemy—revenge and devastation, we!

One last time, hear Clarker upon that hill. Almost like laughter, that sound: Ha! Ha! Ha! His body quivered with plosive bursts, his face a cone of wet merriment: "Today, gentlemen," he seemed to cry, "death today!" Twenty-two hours out of twenty-four we dreaded these twice daily assaults, but when that moment arrived, exhilaration rushed through us as Clarker sounded the advance. We felt as if we had been born for the exclusive joy of these attacks, every fiber in us simultaneously crying out, "At last, holy might, at last!" *That* was the alchemy he performed with his voice, transmuting us from lead into martial gold.

Alas, Joseph Clarker, gentle spirit and god of war—for one instant twice a day, I could be no prouder than to wade thigh-deep in shit into senseless endless combat against an almost mythological adversary. Left scythe, right scythe, nuts and noodle, swipe swipe, bring it on!

Outside of battle, his incomprehensibility was simply annoying. Ask him a direct question, and he just breathed on you. Lucky if you got a syllable in reply. *Yup.* Usually *yup*, but you had no idea if he understood the question. He just stood there expectantly, waiting . . . for what? Clarker was a stupid, stupid fellow.

Seven months on Thisone Rock. On swarm-days, the enemy blocks out the sun: *pool-pah* wind, *pool-pah* sky. With Clarker's blessing upon us, we'll live to see the ships return, to tell them with own mouths what we saw and endured here. Without it, well. We will what will.

Ferocious in war, gentle in peace, beloved by his comrades, Clarker was a man of profound spirituality. You didn't pick it up in his words, but you read it in his eyes. There was an old-soulness about him. Nobody fought this war with a purer union of body and heart, one the flawless extension of the other. When death became inevitable, I've never seen anyone lay down his life with greater tranquility. He accepted the death blow—blows, I guess. Shit, I really should have been watching his flank—with perfect serenity. Death, for Clarker, was no more than a final gate for him to bound through.

If I could say only one thing about Clarker, if I had to sum him up in a single word, it would be this: human. Of all the people I've ever known, of all the people I grew up with during my too brief childhood on Beta, of the all brave warriors who have shed their blood with me during their death sentence on Thisone Rock, Clarker was—and I mean this now—bar none, the most human. He could have written the book on humanity. If, God forbid, this war should be lost and our species eradicated, if the only thing that remained to prove we ever existed was a book on humanity which Clarker had written, I would be satisfied.

Let me close quickly. Turns out "Pescium in patches" doesn't mean a thing. Back to "ad saeculum saeculorum" I guess. Farewell, good Clarker. I hope this was in accordance with your religion. Rof rof.

THE DEATH OF ROGER KEAN

WOW. LOOK AT THIS TURNOUT. Roger Kean would have been touched. Even the palisade guard and the west patrol are here. Who's guarding the fort? Ha ha. I'll keep my remarks short so we don't get overrun.

Hey, look how handsome you all look in your ceremonial uniforms, the sloop stains on your collars no more than shadows. Just now as taps played you stood a little straighter, snapped to attention a little crisper. As fitting. A great man has passed today: this morning the trench aphid finally surrendered him from its digestive tract. But just as Achilles wrought indignity upon the body of Hector, pride of Troy, before returning him to his family for burial, we can now grant the remains of Roger Kean due honor.

If we were on Beta, the traffic corridors would now be

flooded with mourners, the fences outside the Kean estate a siege wall of condolences. This funeral would have been carried on every news channel, the images broadcast into every home in every shaft-domestic. The most aged and feeble in even the poorest households, having not dragged themselves to their feet in decades, would have called to those nearest to prop them up to pay respect to the casket as it traveled in procession across the panel viewer to lie in state.

Here we must scramble to offer the proper tribute, to recreate the solemnity that would have followed Roger Kean's body on Beta. We've constructed banners bearing the Kean family crest—happily, the packing tarp was the right color—we've hollowed out bones and carapaces of the fallen to play a respectable facsimile of the Kean family anthem with full orchestration. (Thank you, Peter Anglewood, for instructing the corps so masterfully on such short notice. Special congratulations to the shrumbug section, your performance was especially tuneful.) It was fortunate we found the score among Roger Kean's effects. Otherwise, we would have had to remember by ear how he whistled the damn thing from reveille until tapping out after evening sloop.

O, those noble strains! That sound is home, isn't it?

Close your eyes while it plays and you see the electrical storms rolling across Beta's surface, you hear the luminous water lapping on the sublunar shores of Beta's fourth moon. Hear those first few phrases, gentlemen, and we've never left the mine shafts where we were reared, where the vim filled our limbs, suited to the toils of the drill, unobjectionable for the labors of war. Hum it once more with me now, will you? Just the last bit. Fee dee doh-de doh...de DOING, feeee der-doh . . . dee . . . daaaah!

When that final note rang pure, bristling with all the strength and moral vigor of Betan life—just a touch of rasp on the Cavendale bone whistle—it wrung the tears from my parched eyes.

(By the way, a rather unreasonable portion of the potable water reserve was used to prepare Roger Kean's body for the ceremony today, I fear I may never afford tears again. Even if the ships return on time in four months, the supply won't last for all of us no matter how harshly we ration. We may have to rely on the bugs to smear a few more of us before then.)

Anyways, here lies Roger Kean: unshakable in his belief in our mission's strategic value. Someone had to be, I guess.

The tactical assessment had recommended a five-to-ten

times larger detachment for a chance at our survival, let alone success. The brass overlooked those recommendations based on its faith in the courage and preparedness of our infantry (that means you guys), the stealth of our deployment methods (remember how we crash-landed here like a meteor?), and the ever-diminishing resolve of the enemy fighters (no comment).

In our numbers, it's impossible we lasted two weeks, let alone seven months. I'm not clever enough to check Doctor Major Cheever Waldorf's math, but by his reckoning, despite two sloop runs a day for two hundred seventeen days (minus six days down with that particularly inventive strain of dysentery), the daily mortality rate for the mantis still lags behind fecundity. That means we haven't made a dent in mantis fighter production capability.

The good news is, killbug authorities here on Thisone seem to remain un-notified of our presence. As far as the bugs are concerned, we operate, in the shantytown of bugland. We could write the words, "Space mammals here!" across the sky with the mutilated carcasses of locals without even getting a write-up in the local newspaper. No one here gives a fuck what we do.

But listening to Roger Kean speak, you'd think the

whole war rested upon our shoulders. "Once more into the sloop! For the species!" Shh, don't giggle. Remember what he used to call us, with tears in his eyes? "My comrades, my brethren, my . . ." Wait for it. "My . . . humans!" We shouldn't laugh, Roger Kean newly dead and all, but wasn't it Roger Kean, who lies half-turdified before us who said, "If anyone wears a long face to my funeral, I shall never speak to him again?" No? Not Roger Kean?

Well, it was somebody.

Roger Kean was a stolid warrior—not the strongest or most cunning, not particularly punctual, never actually led us into the sloop or covered our retreat. But stolid. I say this on account of having no idea what stolid means. Well, what sort of soldier was he? Did Roger Kean even fight? On this rock, we're outnumbered ten billion to one. If he lived this long, he must have shot something by now.

He didn't grow up with us in our shafts-domestic, but we feel we knew him better than we know ourselves. The many and varied achievements of Roger Kean's youth were always upon our lips. When it came to parting the gently glowing waters of Beta's fourth moon, the beauty and ease of his strokes were without peer. As we returned home deliciously sore from our afternoon frolicking scrimmages, images of Roger Kean's own limpid pool-partings dominated the holoscope, his scores for the day frequently matching the league best. Although not among us, Roger Kean was certainly *of* us. We cheered for him. The Kean family lore was part of our upbringing, our history, our pride as Betans. Who here among you cannot recite from memory Roger Kean's third form season highlights at Nordex Academy? Who does not know how with last minute heroics he snatched the prized Gullwaddle Cup from his school's most formidable rival, the Sauerberg Despots? These tales are as fresh in our minds as if we heard them last week.

Roger Kean was Beta's favorite son. We've heard that sentence countless times, but I'm not sure he was even the favorite son of Cameron and Rachel Kean. But Kevin Kean had been on Earth conducting contract negotiations when the bugs ashed it, and the Kean clan would be without honor if it's young men didn't enlist to avenge the Earth, the ragnarite trade, and most importantly Kevin.

The Keans are an ancient Betan family, part of the second wave of colonists, who arrived after ragnarite was discovered but before its full potential as an interworld commodity was understood. The Keans helped develop the market: they strong-armed treaties, gouged out trade routes, and extorted the levy of tariffs. They put Beta on the map after the colony's original investors had written it off as doomed.

During our parents' generation, Beta nearly instigated a war with the rim worlds, one that would have collapsed the ragnarite trade and transformed Beta into another ghost rock. Cameron Kean, with his smooth charm and genteel duplicity, rescued Beta from the brink without a shot being fired. Of course, some say if Cameron Kean hadn't tried to rig the elections on those worlds, the conflict never would have arisen. Nevertheless, that political victory made it possible to negotiate a favorable trade deal with Earth, the one that named Beta as its exclusive ragnarite provider. That made our fortune, allowing the children of simple rag farmers to sweep pan-galactic frolicking championships year after year.

Cameron Kean once gave an impassioned speech on the floor of the Betan Senate about the honor and dignity of the mining tradition, the pride he took in having such intimate ties to the rich veins beneath Beta's surface. Richard Plinth cantankerously swore that if any evidence could be produced that Cameron Kean's father, Mort Kean, could even hold a drill correctly, he would gnaw his own thumbs off. This created a shitstorm when pundits began digging through the archives to see if any such evidence existed. One photo showed Mort Kean holding a drill tentatively, like he was playing an oboe. An outmoded but legitimate technique, we're told. Staunch supporters of the Kean family began demanding Dick Plinth's thumbs, even offering him bottles of relish on the steps of the Capitol. It didn't matter what party you belonged to, the sadism of the political theater was too entertaining to ignore. Ultimately, Dick Plinth got to keep his thumbs, but only after an expensive PR campaign saved his career.

Of course, the whole thing had been ridiculous: no fool would believe Mort Kean had ever put in a day's work in the mine. But after months of scathing attack and physical imperilment, Dick Plinth took the incident personally. He vowed the next time a Kean family member put a foot in his mouth, he'd make sure it got swallowed.

A funny story, but we know better than to laugh! After Earth was destroyed, Cameron Kean chaired the committee responsible for overseeing military recruitment across the Alliance. Despite the urgency manifest by a shrinking frontier, regional governments failed to meet their quotas by greater and greater margins. Around that time, our troops first encountered the mantis fighters, and the nastiness of their attack soon became proverbial. Swipe swipe, pate and privates! When questioned about the dwindling infantry, Cameron Kean, with uncharacteristic candor, lamented that no one in their right mind would enlist knowing at any moment he might see double-scythed mantises swarming over the ridge.

Dick Plinth pounced. He created political pressure for a military operation to infiltrate and destroy the mantis factories, thereby eliminating the recruitment obstacle. Not only would this enable the brave men of the Alliance to heed the call of duty, but it would help his old friend, Cameron Kean, so beleaguered at this critical hour. After a few months of fomented hysteria, the public took the mantis threat seriously enough that Roger Kean himself was forced to volunteer for the campaign.

While waiting out the *pool-pah* under the storm shelter, we've often discussed whether this mission was botched on purpose, the sabotage taking place in the office of Richard Plinth, aimed at the Kean family. We have imagined some sycophantic staff officer from the Ministry of War projecting a map of the galaxy for Plinth's inspection, all known mantis factories labeled. The staff officer, a sniveler with frayed epaulets on his shoulder, says, "Choose. Choose where Roger Kean will lose his life." A shudder of pleasure courses through Dick Plinth—

he has a hard on, it thrills him so much—but his face betrays no satisfaction. He waves a hand, nonchalant.

"Does it matter? Any of them. This one."

The staff officer licks his lips. "Designation 2W4-Gamma3. Would you like to give it a name?"

Dick Plinth, cantankerous as ever, repeats, "*This one!*"

Although the story is Hemlock's invention, some version of it must be true.

We're told the proper pronunciation of this rock is Tee-SOHN-uh, an old Alpachioux word for "ambush point." Before our deployment, I had never heard of the Alpachioux, but after three days of nosing through archives, I finally found them listed in a catalog of North American native tribes. None of their language appears to be documented, not even "Thisone." But who knows? The bugs have blown the Earth's anthropological records to bits.

But how could even someone harboring a blood grievance dare to hijack this vital mission? After all, the mantis fighters are the primary obstacle to victory—and hominid salvation! Their savage attack culls our courage even in face of annihilation. Our men hear "Left scythe right scythe, map and man-berries," they put on dresses and cower under their beds!

Die in a graviton tank and your neural system catches fire, you slow burn from your spine to your extremities—but our men are brave. Get stuck in a singularity sub when its horizon cracks, the temporal shift is so violent, none of your internal organs will have ever existed at the same time—yet young men still eagerly volunteer. But tell them there's a bug that cuts your cock off as a reflex, well, suddenly the preservation of the human species isn't so important.

As if egregious crotch injury was the deterrent, and not that our survival is subject to the whim of petty political vendettas!

So, the brass sends in a crack unit—us!—to fight 'em in the fuckhills. To die beyond the rim where no one will hear our last shit-stifled howls of dickless agony. Twice a goddamn day in genital peril. Comrades-in-arms, it would take at least five runs a day at our current kill rate to make a dent in mantis fighter production. Analysis suggests the bugs don't even value mantis fighters: their commanders deploy them haphazardly into the fray to maintain confusion between waves of more elite units. Nuisance troops. That's who we're fighting.

But who better to send than the Betans who spend their boyhood crawling underground, who spelunk better than fish swim or birds fly? After a week, they'll know the tunnels better than the bugs who dug them!

When we received orders to ship out here, I heard so much of this nonsense, I thought we were going on vacation. Lucky us! They forgot to mention the weather patterns are savage enough to rival anything on Beta's surface: not just shit storms, but shiticanes and shitnados. Nor'shitters. El shityo. But I handle it just like I did on Beta: a pair of rubber boots and a slicker. How many of us have ever spent more than a few hours on Beta's blasted surface?

"Doesn't the night sky here on Thisone remind us of home?" asks Roger Kean. "When we gaze up at the broad swath of human stars, don't we recall what we are fighting for?"

No, Roger Kean, only when I look down. Between my legs, I mean. Are you suggesting that the lethal shadow-wasps as they bank and swoop beneath the cloud cover remind me of the wangbats that flitter from moonrim to moonrim on Beta of a clear summer night? No. Are you fucking insane? No! Children *pet* wangbats at the zoo, their parents video their first wangbat ride. Do wangbats ever eviscerate the entire south patrol during their mating cycle? Do *wangbats* ever mix our corpses with vomit and spunk then pile the mixture into tumuli that dot the Cavendale Ridge? No, they do not!

When Roger Kean hears this, he senses the Thisone romance is over, so he discards pretense and levels with us:

"Does it seem to you we are here just for appearances? So be it. If appearance turns back the killbug horde, neither you nor I will have toiled in vain. Throughout history, men no more brave, with no less to lose, have willingly sacrificed for the same reason you and I give of ourselves here, to show our cause is one worth fighting for. It is this burden of proof that you and I bear every morning, every evening into the sloops. We are told that among the killbug swarm, there is a danger so horrifying, some men shudder to chance upon it. Then let *us* chance upon it, twice a day, every day, three times on Christmas, to demonstrate to all that our species' safety has been entrusted to men who balk at nothing."

Preach it, Roger Kean! You might just be inspiring someone.

He continues:

"At this moment, in homes and town halls and in the highest chambers of hominid government, cynics are trying to denigrate the courage and resolve of our fighting men, they are pessimistic about the capability of our leadership, about the strength and efficiency of our army and fleet. They recommend putting off the struggle and perils of war for as long as possible. But we Betans are loathe to pass up an opportunity to defend the values we treasure. Our faith is not shaken by their words. No suffering or fatigue, not even the threat of mutilation diminishes our love for humanity and human civilization.

"Some of you think the mantis isn't important enough to journey this far into hostile space, beyond the reach of communication with our families and allies. I agree. It is not. But it is not the mantis we fight here. Back home, much more dangerous adversaries are gathering strength: cynicism, pessimism, fatalism. Foes which threaten the welfare of future generations, threaten the rightful place of humanity in the galaxy, threaten the legacy our ancestors devoted their lives to fostering and have since handed down to us.

"Have no illusion: the twin blades of cynicism and opportunism also have the power to de-face and un-man us, and the disfigured husk they leave behind is far more unrecognizable than the work of any mantis.

"Some of you may lament that the burden of defeating so abstract an opponent has fallen upon us. I do not. The annals of human history are rife with individuals who lament their lives have lacked any meaning or purpose. Then let us count ourselves fortunate that purpose and meaning have come so effortlessly to our door. What many have spent lifetimes seeking in science, philosophy, and religion, we find before us every hour in duty. Shall we not then look up at the clear night sky and see in each star a call to consequence? In days past, when they were lost asea, our ancestors looked to those same stars for guidance. But on this night, my comrades, it is those lights who turn to us standing upon this shore, to shepherd *them* through the darkness and lead *them* once more to safe harbor. To be set apart in honor, to bear the torch and show the way for countless others, who, then, is luckier than us?"

A rousing speech changes everything. When Roger Kean speaks, I confess I am enraptured. I think, geez, if things had gone only a little different, I wouldn't have gotten the chance to come out here. I breathe deeply and think, God, that stench makes me want to vomit bile. But for a moment, I *do* feel lucky; for the life of me I have no idea why, but the thrill rushes down to my toes. Because Roger Kean is speaking to me, the Kean family Roger Kean, Nordex champion frolicker, he!

Mortal and digestible, both. Ask me if I liked him. But I'm almost giddy the privilege has fallen to me today to say a few words at his funeral which, had it been held on Beta, the traffic corridors would now be flooded with mourners, the fences outside the Kean estate a siege wall of condolences . . . Oh, I did that part.

As I said last time, we each have our reasons for wanting to see ourselves off this rock. Roger Kean had his political ambitions. Vote for Roger Kean the Mantis Fighter, who took the struggle to the darkest corner of the galaxy, who conquered the most fearsome foe, who came back unspoiled because his face was pretty and his testicles solid steel.

In an alternate universe where he doesn't die on Thisone but survives to run for office, that Roger Kean never winks on his campaign posters. Hey look, an honest-to-God not winker! Unlike candidates today who stand there unwinking like snake oil salesmen whom someone has trained not to wink, Roger Kean has had the winking bred out generations ago. His left eye is sealed open like on the busts of the ancients, from a time when politicians were called statesmen and buildings were made to stand forever. Men's words may decay over time, but unwinking Roger Kean speaks in inscriptions as marble stelae rise rumbling from the ground to take dictation.

With him among us, we weren't carrying out just one

more mission, we were participating in history. Roger Kean stood as the pivot upon which history turned, and we were there. Even the death or survival of the human race seems trivial except to the extent it matters in the story of Roger Kean. Although he wasn't our commander, we were Roger Kean's men. Whenever you spoke and Roger Kean listened, it was his listening—not your speaking!—which held the spotlight. And when he spoke to you, he looked directly into you and melded with you, and you and he were the only ones in the galaxy. Nothing could happen elsewhere while he held your gaze. It was like a spell.

Still, I don't think Roger Kean could see you, not really. None of us were ever substantial in the mind of Roger Kean. The storm of his existence swirled at a level of complexity far above any of us. People like us dissolve into particles up there.

The only thing Roger Kean ever saw was his own legacy, and for this reason he did not dread death like some of us do. Conscious of how this moment is both the past's future and the future's past, he did not fear any particular destiny because he believed—correctly too, which is what infuriates me—that history, whatever history shall remain, shall remember this war in terms of Roger Kean. But the many who fought and died beside him will no doubt be forgotten.

Somehow Roger Kean managed to stand at the center of everything.

Why does history stick to some and not to others? Why do our struggles, our yearnings, our agonies remain insignificant even at the moments when the entire galaxy roars with our lungs, pounds with our hearts, flows with our blood? Why will Thisone Rock forever be where Roger Kean fought and died, yet we, Lions of Beta, will never have been here at all?

In preparing this speech, I decided to go through Roger Kean's personal journals—you know, those ones he kept so he had an excuse never to speak to us? I opened the pages at random, hoping to let Roger Kean give his own eulogy. Who could do it better than the man himself?

I discovered he heaps praise on the members of this unit, especially a young man named Barry Hofstadter. Remember him? Burnt up on arrival. I don't think a molecule of him reached the ground. But there are pages upon pages about him in there. All heroics and self-sacrifice, this PFC Hofstadter. Why not one of you? Hell, why not me? But when this journal is published after the war, we'll all be fighting tooth-and-nail to prove we knew

Hofstadter best, the dumb bastard too stupid to check if his drop seat was sealed properly.

You should read these entries, though. Roger Kean makes daily assessments of our mission's progress. "Complete eradication of bug hill imminent." He wrote that about the orange mantes from Fuckhill Tiger Sutra. Yeah, the oranges, those dread bastards! Kill one, and I swear, two more leap out of the carcass and bite your nuts off. We wouldn't last three weeks if we attacked Tiger Sutra. Well, flip forward a few pages. "Unfortunately, an avalanche has cut off our access to Tiger Sutra's sloop or we'd be using their hive as a base of operations within a week." Fascinating! Please continue, Roger Kean. "Projecting our current kill rate over the rest of our sojourn on T., Command can expect a twenty percent reduction in mantis fighters at the front." Twenty percent! I'll look forward to that!

Reading his journal, I was so moved by the strength of our resolve, the quality of our leadership, I half-overlooked that none of it happened that way. But that's how Roger Kean wrote it, so maybe I misremember. Hey look, here's Hofstadter fighting beside us all along!

Well, Roger Kean is dead, and he left his data encryption open, so I've done us all a service: whenever he mentions of one of you by name, I've made Roger Kean struck dumb by the size of that man's genitals. From now on, Roger Kean will have spent his days on Thisone really, really impressed by your cocks. How brave of you loin-heavy gentlemen to confront those psycho-circumcisers with such outrageously proportioned targets. I can't guarantee an editor won't notice my little interpolations, but until one does, history will remember us knocking cannonballs about knee-high.

If humanity survives this war, history will owe us something. I'd much prefer it recall that when faced with annihilation, humanity saw fit to throw us into the teeth of destiny just to settle the score on some childish political rivalry. But failing that, I'll settle for a giant free-swinging scrotum! The mantes rear up in fear at the sight of it. Hey, they're mantes: the one thing they understand is getting fucked to death. Ahoy hoy!

As children, who among us imagined we'd while away our prime at the far end of the galaxy polishing turds as if our lives depended on it? The venomous merdaddies are terrified of reflected light, but everything exposed to the sandstorms corrodes in a matter of days, and the only renewable material available to maintain a shiny perimeter is shit. But bug shit, which literally rains from the sky, won't do for the job—only human shit will suffice. Hey, we gotta do a shit drive! Brother Private, can you donate a turd to the western defense? Then, of course, someone's got to make that shit shine—that's the point. Well, did Roger Kean ever do polish detail? He was assigned countless times, but we always traded him for it. "Oi, Roger Kean, pull a string for us, pretty please. We'll polish your shit for you." And ol' Roger Kean, magnanimous as ever, looked out over the sea of hopeful faces that crowded his bunk. Who oh who would he let shine his shit for him today?

Was there any reason Roger Kean should hold more clout out than any of us here on Thisone? But it was so. Why, just this morning I was still wording my petition to shine shit for Roger Kean when I remembered. Oop, dead. So today I bear a different duty, to polish the Roger Kean turd orally—to make it bright enough with my words to keep all the merdaddies in the galaxy at bay.

Because, I tell you, comrades-in-arms, I cannot say precisely what virtues the goo sack in front of us once had which the rest of us lack, but our plight is definitely gloomier without him. Today, gentlemen, we are imperiled. Today, our own allies, even our own families, deem us less deserving to survive because we did not drive back the ravenous jaws of the trench aphids with our bodies, because we did not sate them first with our own flesh, because we failed our sacred trust to shield the Favorite Son of Beta. Even we do not question the wisdom of this. So let's all throw ourselves under the crush of the hover transport. We're here on a mission, to eradicate the imagined recruitment threat posed by a small number of mantis fighters, but what does it matter in a galaxy without Roger Kean, champion in the venerable art of the frolic?

Out of the dozens of funerals I've attended since we landed here, this one is the most elaborate, this one has the largest band and the most banners. The banquet we'll attend later has the heaviest tables, despite the strict rationing it will force upon us. Some of you sewed yourselves new uniforms just for this ceremony, because even with most of the galaxy between us and Beta you're still afraid of embarrassing the folks back home. You should have seen Doctor Cheever Waldorf in his lab tailoring those spiffy threads he's got on, as if he was under the gun. But nothing too fancy either, right? Don't wanna upstage the bride at the wedding, so to speak.

Look around yourselves, gentlemen. Do you see a face among us to whom you do not owe your lives to at least a dozen times over? Now, ask yourselves: does anyone here believe that Roger Kean felt that you—not the human species, not the fate of civilization—that *you* were worth defending with his own life? The truth now, we won't judge.

Oh, what does any of that matter? Today, thou art poop, Son of Beta. Sleep well, sweet prince.

Let's eat, gentlemen. Save me a slice of ham. Ad saeculum saeculorum. Amen.

THE DEATH OF PETER ANGLEWOOD

S HALL I START WITH A POEM?

> Peedlebugs are orange
> Their mandibles red
> Their tummies got fuller
> Peter Anglewood dead

The meter's a bit broke, but so was Pete's face. Cracked like a walnut down the middle. Standing behind him, I could see both earholes at once.

. . . And what clever ears they'd been, giving rudder to the perfect pitched melodies that sailed from his golden throat aside the luminous lakes of Beta's fourth moon. There in the murk-watered lagoons where the spotted-kettlepip seed their roe, the boys and girls frolicked for favors, their svelte bodies breaching the surface like wisps of comet hair. Particulate light glinted off resin-rich droplets, and fragrant nightkelp perfumed their squealing exhalations.

The beauty of Betan youth, insouciant in the mine shafts, knew no rival save the balmy psalms with which Peter Anglewood praised it. Like a cunning co-evolution, the splendor of each chased the other to heights yet unknown. Never has the galaxy borne witness to a more handsome pairing of sound and subject, a more supple balance of limb and lyric than the song and swimmers who flailed and frolicked along the kelp-tressed shore.

O cruel Thisone! It was there on Beta's sublunar shores Anglewood ought to have whiled away his years, paying honor to Beta's budding flower, generation after generation into his pervy old-agedom. (Because, let's face it, crowning the bloom of youth in metered song is sorta creepy at any age, and Anglewood was already doing it at twelve.) But without peer he yoked sound to honeyed sound, seamlessly stringing syllables for both sonority and sense (although occasionally overindulging in alliteration).

Perhaps this was the sort of beauty the horrors of war are made to destroy. Because when such a consummate artist crystallizes a fleeting moment into an eternal thunderclap of language and music, well, time itself may grind to a halt. As he stood on Beta's lunar shores, Anglewood was hurling wrenches into the cogs of growth and decay.

Before Earth was ashed, young Peter had dedicated himself to celebrating beauty in both its physical and moral forms. He believed, though he was only a poet, that he understood beauty's character, that he could recognize its mark upon the flesh and in the soul. Beauty, he said, was warm in the underglow of the lunar pools. It whistled in the rumreed that bowed gently under bracing cavern breezes. It lay heavy upon the lower branches of the nubility tree where frolickers hung their gaily-shed unisex water onesies before engaging their shapely bodies in blithesome water-partings. It was beauty which Anglewood heard in the heaven-seeking high-scoring peals of laughter that blew the judges' tally spheres to spin madly, that provoked the referees to cry penalty! "Too *much* joy!" they scolded, "too *much* merriment!" He gratified himself in the almost illicit revelry that characterized the post-match celebrations in honor of Beta's pioneers, the exuberant exchange of favors offered up to the numen of our ancestors.

On Beta, Anglewood's verses were the bronze plate upon which our ephemeral glory was engraved. How adorable, how common. It took the destruction of Earth to force Peter to not to shy from the pocks and bumps and greasy bits in the galaxy's texture, irregularities that create friction, generating the heat he needed to scald the galaxy into exciting new misshapes. Over the years of strife, this war refashioned Anglewood into someone whose words would force his listeners to rear and falter, to make them forget their answers to the fundamental questions—a true artist. Peter slowly evolved from a mere singer of songs into a refashioner of worlds.

In the war's first days, Anglewood had believed it was in the frolic that beauty lay and where our virtue was revealed, not in the gruesome martial meeting of man and bug, the arbitrary mechanics of their mutual annihilation. What is combat? he asked. Here one man swells with youthful vim; there one insect exults in its newly-molted triptych carapace. They stand opposed, eye to compound eye. Trusting the strength of their scant years, which their progenitors have augmented by the power of technology or the evolution of adrenal glands, they launch at each other and strike—leaving what? A stain. What is it all for? Every poignant arc of their lives, all the triumph and tender tragedy, has ended in the spin of a blender. Not enough body to bury, and what falls to the ground poisons the soil for generations. For only this did our parents bear and nurture us: a barren patch of earth, a few minutes of eulogy?

When Beta swore a blood oath to avenge Earth, personal honor and stringent recruitment quotas left us no choice but to enlist. Peter, too, volunteered, but not to fight. "I bring no weapons," he said, "save my voice and my minstrel's heart. Also, a fat sack of positron grenades, in case it gets hairy. But let there be no doubt, I'm here to conduct a war against war."

He was going to sing it to death. On our first mission, then-Lieutenant Croop let him take his instruments into combat. Anglewood stood atop a hill with his theretar and his UV harp while on the field below, man and bug were smashed in the fate-accelerator. A third of our regiment got smeared in the first five minutes. For every note Peter blew on his harp that day, twenty thousand lives were lost. The power coils on his theretar were so splattered with viscera, the instrument wouldn't even sound.

Later when our shattered ranks were reconstituted, I said to Pete, "Huh. Looks like war won."

That was the young idealist who left Beta. Yet these last months on Thisone we have fought in the shadow of an Anglewood demon. Among our ranks, no one was more seeped in bug gore. That thickened rind of congealed bug bits had not formed due to prowess at arms, but because he glued them on every morning before sloop. He adorned his body with knickknacks salvaged from enemy corpses, choosing his war trophies less for their ability to make him appear menacing than their so-called symbolic significance.

Peter was a terror to behold—or at least a source of momentary confusion—and when he discharged his weapon, he also unloaded a volley of verses: lyric, sonnets, madrigals, ballads cantos and terza rimas, elegiacs, eclogues, limericks, palindromes and tongue twisters, dirges, ditties, doggerel, and what I assume were bits of scat. "Poetry has never killed anyone," he always said, "but that's no reason you shouldn't try."

Oh, what did it matter that our war was unwinnable? The essence of beauty, Peter now claimed, was the inevitability of decay. For the body, this meant old age and putrefaction; for action, it was expressed in futility. Precisely because our efforts here on Thisone were daily forays into suffering and frustration, he found satisfying elegance in it.

As our point man, he made a fantastic amount of noise, which, who knows, may have interfered with the bugs' ability to communicate. Holy hell, that voice could carry.

But at least by keeping him where we could see him, we could shout him down before he performed any premeditated stupidity.

Anglewood led us into combat with song, and because he was poor at this, we fought. I felt compelled to bring down an Armageddon just to cover my embarrassment. That man attached bug antennae to his helmet! I swear, every world government should select a poet laureate, to shame its people to compensate.

So what happened? What compelled him across the Anglewoodian bridge between these two Peters? As we know, he recorded the whole journey for us in his watershed work, "My Conversion to the Muse of Mars," a poem of fifteen thousand lines. As I skimmed over it last night to make selections to include in today's remarks, a sudden tunneling tremor caused the only extant copy to fall into the incinerator. Yes, I know, what a loss. Well, I suppose I can recount the story myself, only it won't be rhymed or metered. But perhaps I can toss in a few poetic turns to produce confusion in the right places. Here goes.

We were on Cayenne Rock when that slaw locust crawled into camp crippled and blinded. Despite its intent to fight to the death, Major Calvin Hoot, the Psi Ward's Director of Enhanced Ask-No-Questions Techniques on

Cayenne, ordered it subdued and taken prisoner. Considering its pitiful condition, it hardly seemed worth the Director's time to not find out what it didn't know, but rules is rules. The Psi Ward put the locust on neurotoxins and acid damage for the sake of form.

Doctor Lieutenant Cheever Waldorf had just completed his study at the West Galactic Anthroentomology Institute where he had participated in research and development for a real-time human-bug universal translator. So far, the Institute had documented eighty-seven killbug languages, but still required speech samples from most species. For this, it would rely on the aid of the military to make native bug speakers available for study.

Slaw locusts were infrequent on disputed rocks, so Cheever leapt at the opportunity to wesearch this specimen, even in its compromised state. Estimating he could compile a comprehensive lexicon of the slaw locust's language within a few months, Cheever petitioned the Psi Ward to have it handed over to him. Once it contributed to the compendium of bug languages, Cheever would return the prisoner so they could not ask it all the questions they liked. But Director Hoot claimed he had protocols to follow, and unfortunately the Lt. Dr. could not be facilitated.

134

Cheever protested. "The Amalgam of Hominid Scientists has determined the Institute's pwoject is paramount in bringing this war to an agreeable conclusion. Besides, in our experience, most bugs have limited linguistic capacity, some fewer than a thousand words. Where to pile the shit, how high the shit should be piled, that sort of thing. Judging by its simplistic behavior, I anticipate the prisoner's language will be a rudimentary one. If necessary, Director, I can pledge my study will be completed within a month."

Director Hoot made a gesture indicating his hands were tied. "With due respect to the Institute's pwoject, Lieutenant Second Doctor Waldorf, the Security Command Council has assigned the not asking of questions the highest priority. However, to assure you this decision is not intended as a slight against you or the Scientific Amalgam, the Psi Ward is graciously granting you leave to conduct your investigation in conjunction with non-inquires, so long as you can offer assurances the subject will suffer and not die without permission."

Cheever left the Director's office in a huff. "That's wesearch for you," he muttered. "An *egwegious* abuse of authority!"

Nevertheless, knowing the Psi Ward's propensity to

indefinitely belabor the questions it didn't ask, he believed it might still be possible to compile a tentative lexicon before the subject was too incapacitated to provide sample speech. The prisoner appeared a more sophisticated species than he had represented to Director Hoot, but he doubted its vocabulary would be more than three or four times greater than his estimate.

The slaw locust, however, turned out to be surprisingly loquacious.

The decryption routines on Cheever's equipment identified a staggering six thousand potential phonemes. After eliminating a few hundred of them as burps, wheezes, and other bodily noises, it eventually managed to congeal the remaining audial soup into distinct linguistic terms. But the real hurdle proved to be the syntax.

"I don't understand," Cheever complained to no one who was listening. "The Institute has spent the last twenty years developing algorithms for codifying the bugs' linguistic structures—the methodology for cracking these nuts has long been established! But on this particular bug, I'm getting nowhere. Generally, killbug speech is *heroically* precise, but this subject's discourse appears vague and ambiguous, almost deliberately so. Also, the words have an extraordinary range of meanings, but the way the subject chooses between them doesn't seem even *remotely* context dependent. I'm at my wits' end!"

Cheever thought he might make headway if he could determine the slaw locust's place in the killbugs' social hierarchy. But infuriatingly, he couldn't decode the trillburp he was convinced was meant to signify its caste. The locust had rejected fighter, burden bearer, digger, piler, depiler, larva feeder, stationary target practice, munitions swallower, artillery pooper, mobile target practice, mine bug, and rock melter.

Cheever doubted the locust served any high-order function or else the bugs would have sent a rescue/kill mission, but it couldn't hurt to ask. It also rejected general, hive architect, rock inseminator, water gelatinization specialist, slop pile engineer, adrenal modifier, genetic shaman, death orgy planner, nanobug research and developer. Nevertheless, the bug seemed to be assuring Cheever it had an even more vital role.

"Delusionist of grandeur?" Cheever suggested in frustration.

"Yes," said the bug, "Yes!"

Cheever smirked. "We got one of those too." Licking his lips, he summoned an MP. "Get Private Anglewood in here. Maybe this bug's a poet."

When Pete was escorted in, Cheever instructed him to introduce himself to the prisoner through the translator.

Pete giggled like a kid in a toy store, told to take anything he wants.

"Greetings to our most esteemed guest, reputed Fear of the Gongo and Terror of the Keprich Prong. It is I, Peter of the—"

The translator box exploded with a deafening screech and static.

Cheever was exasperated. "The codec is stwuggling as is, Anglewood. Speak plainly to it. We are still at the baby talk stage."

But the locust whizzlepopped in response to Peter and the translator crackled with human speech. "Grizzled death horde swarm carrion. Flatulence."

"Bless you," said Peter. "Many honors be upon your grave."

"Anglewood, talk like a person, please. This is for science!"

"Good noise," said the locust. "Murder. Tribute whale, generation muck up slurp."

This went on for twenty minutes. It was difficult to tell if the nonsensical outputs were the result of imperfections in the codec or of the equally nonsensical inputs, but

Cheever couldn't deny Anglewood was eliciting the first enthusiastic response from the locust.

Cheever had previously programmed some modifications to the translator's algorithmically generated rules, but on a hunch, he now commented out those functions and rebooted the box.

"All right, you two," Cheever said. "Poeticize! Give us the fancy stuff!"

The room filled with a deafening litany of inarticulate burp-wheezes, gurgle-farts, and cough-whistles. Then the bug spoke too. Ha!

As Anglewood recited, the translator spat out its conjectural bug jabber—chirps, pops, and static. Gradually, the slaw locust's battered lump roused itself and it began to trill rhythmically.

Cheever understood nothing yet coming back through the speaker, but he was ecstatic. This could be a watershed moment. In the years he'd spent studying killbug anthropology, he had been desperately seeking evidence the bugs possessed linguistic culture. Many anthro-entomologists, including members of his own wesearch team, doubted the bugs used language for anything other than utilitarian purposes: filth piling instructions, military maneuvers, procreative clusterfucking. Arguing from silence, they said the lack of linguistic culture demonstrated a fundamental incompatibility between our civilizations.

But now! By all appearances, this slaw locust was playing word games with Peter. Slumped in a mutilated heap before him could be the first documented instance of a bug *poet*. The field of wesearch born that day had the potential to bridge the cultural gap between humans and killbugs. It was possible, Cheever believed, that despite the dramatic differences in our physiognomy, the barriers between us were chiefly cosmetic, and that our aims were fundamentally similar and not in conflict. Cheever estimated that with enough effort, this discovery could produce not only a cessation of hostilities, but down the line, even social integration.

Poor Cheever.

He had a problem, however. The slaw locust, reasonably believing Cheever to be part of the Psi Ward's torture squad, was extremely reluctant to participate in his study. So, for a second time, Cheever petitioned for a cessation to the interrogations not being conducted. For a second time, he was denied. The Psi Ward even complained that Cheever's wesearch was contaminating the locust's lack of response to questions not being asked.

Not yet giving up, Cheever conjectured that in the

presence of Peter Angelwood, professional pride might compel the locust to dredge up its store of lyric. So Cheever tried to requisition Peter Anglewood as a wesearch assistant, on account of him being of no god damn use for anything else.

"Denied," came the response. Director Hoot regretted Anglewood would not be available for a lab position because he had been court-martialed for shitty soldiery and unforgivable musicianship. The raids on Corkplug Hive last week had been an unqualified failure, and it was felt it would be a morale booster for the Psi Ward if they got to kill someone.

"This is cwazy!" Cheever cried.

"Don't get fwazzled," said Director Hoot.

"I'm not frazzled," managed Cheever.

"Of course not. Anyway, the evidence was ironclad: by any standard, Anglewood certainly does suck. I'm afraid he's been sentenced to be shot."

Cheever and Anglewood had never been friends, but Cheever saw no reason to surrender a valuable tool to the firing squad, especially if this might change the course of the war. Calling in some favors, he managed to delay Peter's execution on a technicality. Then he arranged for Peter to be held in a cell adjacent to the slaw locust, hoping that for a fellow poet and prisoner, the slaw locust might overlook Anglewood's humanness and begin to confide in him. Peter was allowed his musical instruments and Cheever's translator was "accidentally" left on at night, so the two could communicate.

Would you believe they didn't make a peep to each other for days? Despite their previous joy at discovering another of their kind, artistic jealousy set in as soon as they were placed across from each other. Each believed the other incapable of appreciating the merit of their work, yet feared the other was conspiring to steal it anyway!

Privately, each asked to be moved. "I don't feel free to practice my art," they complained.

Cheever was weally, weally angwy.

"What art?" he demanded. "You are condemned to die. Both of you! You wanna play your theratar? You wanna blow your butt whistle? Do it for each other, or not at all!"

One night, believing the slaw locust had passed out from the agony of what it hadn't been asked, Peter began to sing. Wearily the bug lifted its head and turned up a scorched ear to listen. In its pain-induced delirium, the sound of Peter buzzing over the translator reminded the bug of the day it witnessed its parents slaughtered before its eyes. Soft driblets came oozing from its empty sockets.

The broken mandible vibrated, and other gassy orifices hummed as nostalgia welled deep within its carapace. Then in the dark stench of that tiny cell, tentatively at first but with growing confidence, for the first time in history, a killbug made available to human ear the great epics of Acrididae.

"Excellent," said Cheever the next day. "We're finally documenting some killbug culture here! But the larger the compendium of verses we put together, the more we can *wearn* about them. Anglewood, I want you to see if you can get him to really open up to you. Tell some personal stories. Try to be his friend. Give him a name!"

So, the slaw locust became "Sledge." This was Peter's approximation of what he assumed the bug was calling himself. In truth, that unpleasant sound he kept making was not a vocalization but vapor rising from aeration holes on account of acid burns he received day and night from the ask-no-questions squad. But prisoners are called whatever their captors choose, so Sledge did not object. He just continued shrieking involuntarily in his cage like a lobster.

Anglewood, for his part, sang to Sledge about the Betan tradition of competitive frolic, the beauty of parting the surface of sublunar pools with powerful strokes from supple limbs. He described the fishes and the algae, the smart streaks of ragnarite resin across the bare bodies of swimmers. He listed all the scoring rules and penalties, recounted the post-frolic favor exchanges in excruciating detail. Not even the Psi Ward could have yammered on so sadistically, but the damaged locust hung on every word.

"How many are killed in a frolic?" Sledge asked with enthusiasm.

"Well," Anglewood replied, "sometimes a Betan youth has an aneurysm from frolicking too hard . . ."

"Not accidental deaths. How many are slaughter-killed?"

"Why would anyone be killed?"

"Because you call it a frolic. Frolic means killing, does it not?"

"No. Frolic means play."

"I do not understand," said Sledge, "you have said, 'Frolic does not mean to kill, it means to kill.' The translator must error."

But of course, there was no mistake. In the language of the slaw locust, "kill" and "play" were the same word.

This was no small discovery. From this source of momentary confusion followed the most monumental

144

anthro-entomological breakthrough of our time. Here's what Cheever learned.

I'll give it to you prosaical, without the anacreontic dimeters.

Murder, in addition to being the chief form of recreation for killbugs, has an even deeper spiritual significance. Citing many traditional songs, Sledge explained how death-making was the sacred mission imparted to them by the Opifex, the primordial creator god who with his hands and voice built the entirety of the cosmos. Upon completion, he surveyed his work, from its infinite breadth to its infinitesimal detail, and found mistakes at every turn. He fell into despair.

To atone for his myriad failures, he gathered all his remaining ingenuity and strength to construct one final artifice, the First Queen. She was his most perfect creation. The Opifex crowned his triumph by removing the matter-shaping voice from his throat and offering it to her on the tip of his finger. She devoured it, finger and all, and without further hesitation, tore Opifex limb from limb. As she consumed him piece by piece, she laid the eggs from which all killbugs are descended.

The moral of the story: Just as it had been the divine task of the Opifex to make the universe, the killbugs believe the solemn duty falls upon them to *unmake* it, to sing in counterpoint to the Creator of All: to match peak with trough and trough with peak until the whole of the cosmos rests in the breath-quenching beauty of silence.

Therefore, for the bug, killing is the perfect expression of joy. It consummates a life of love and prayer; it represents the strength, will, and faith to close the circuit of life; it demonstrates due reverence for the awesome power of decay.

Looking up from the transcription of this discussion, Cheever poured himself a drink.

The slaw locust explained to Anglewood how this murder-ethos is exemplified in the time-honored tradition of the death orgy. To commemorate the devouring of Opifex and the ascension of the First Queen as Negatress of the Cosmos, the older generations joyously slaughter one another in the sight of the young. These witnesses are encouraged to devour the twitching carcasses of their elders. To be slaughtered as part of the death orgy is believed to bring honor to the Core Hive, just as it is both a privilege and a sign of reverence to eat a beloved neighbor butchered on the sacred sands of the orgy arena.

According to Sledge, all killbugs are born murderers, but each culture has its own sacrament to foster reverence for death-making among its people. For the slaw locusts, this is a coming-of-age ritual called Confinement where seven nymphs are buried together in a cell for a month without food. During this period, strong bonds form between the youngsters, partly due to intimate quarters but mostly because they are forced to eat one of their fellows to survive. The nymphs, yet unaccustomed to slaughter, must settle amongst themselves on how to choose the devouree.

Fighting is a common method. The last nymph standing wins the right to decide who will be eaten. It is not unheard of for the victor to elect himself. Distributing his strength among his cellmates in this way is seen as multiplying his influence among his peers. Also, the spirit of one's Confinement devouree is typically invoked as a personal fury in future combat, therefore guaranteeing a kind of immortality. That is why this gesture is seen as more self-serving than altruistic.

(Hey, if I was a vomit-piling slaw locust, I'd want to be the first to end my miserable existence too. I say this as a sloop-crawling human.)

In Sledge's circle, the matter was settled by vote prior to the Confinement. The devouree would have the privilege of writing a song in his own memory, which his body-eaters were honor-bound to memorize and sing at the circle's reunions. Sledge's peers chose him on account of his mellifluidity. He composed a brilliant poem about the glory of being slain in the ritual, about how by giving himself in remembrance of the Opifex's own sacrifice, his spirit was guaranteed to return to the state of neutrality that had existed before the birth of the cosmos. He also named the many figures from his ancestry (naturally not in the direct line) who had also shared this honor. A finer devourment song had never been composed.

As such, it roused the jealousy of a devious slaw locust named Benteye.

Hearing the unmatched splendor of Sledge's woofgargles and bleatspots, the wicked Benteye begrudged Sledge the glory of his death among the Confinement circle.

Claiming that he had merely wanted to learn about the illustrious family history of his circle's devouree, Benteye uncovered a long list of villainies and disgustitudes committed by Sledge's ancestors (naturally, all Benteye slanders and fabrications), and published them in the hive square. The heinous allegations included charges of clemency, largess, temperance, and sexual fidelity. Any slaw locust would be indelibly tarnished to devour someone with so many black marks upon his name. The vote had to be retaken. Since Benteye was the one who had spared them this dishonor, it was he who was elected and eaten down to the last protein glop.

How tense for Sledge those long weeks in close quarters among resentful peers. How the putrefying morsels of his false friend turned his stomach. Oh, what a bitter meal! In his intestines, he felt it congeal into a hard stone of sacrilege.

Eventually, Benteye's treachery was revealed and Sledge's family's name restored, but the shame of that month remained with him, forever fixing his unworthiness in his own mind. The trauma made him hate himself so much, he wanted to live forever.

Compassionate elders, who knew firsthand what vicious bastards Sledge's parents had been, took him aside and tried to re-instill in him a youthful yearning for death. They even made him consume special mosses so poisonous the agony would make anyone want to give up the ghost, but nothing helped. Life! Life is what he deserved!

To suffer the full brunt of his indefinite existence, Sledge decided to immerse himself completely in the cultural study of death and killing, the pleasures of which he would never permit himself to partake. He became a killbug bard, undertaking the arduous task of committing to memory thousands of songs, the sacred words of the Queen's children.

Sledge had a natural gift for recitation. His voice was considered powerful and hypnotic among the killbugs. (Even his captors on Cayenne Rock admitted he farted beautifully!) Yet how could he, someone to whom the community would turn for guidance on the path to honorable dismemberment, satisfy his duties when, for him, death had become so abhorrent? The issue weighed heavily on his conscience. Sledge felt like a fraud.

Anglewood confessed he had experienced something similar as a teenager on Beta. At first, he'd been ambivalent toward poetry, but he simply lacked coordination for the frolic. Once, an entire season had passed without him scoring even a splashmo or onesying a single opponent. But a Betan youth belonged no place except by the limpid pools of the fourth moon. He had to do *something* on the shore besides lie there masturbating. So, he started to compose.

Yet even as he praised Beta in song, he wanted nothing more than to be free of it. He found the whole rock unbearable, with its carcinogenic ore, its foul-smelling pools, its bullshit sports, its numberless horde of young people hideously deformed from generations of inbreeding. He felt he'd rather die than think about Beta or her shining youth again.

But over time he found that poetry, that insidiously self-mocking art, buoyed him up. It was a strange addiction: the less he believed what he was saying, the more vehemently he performed it, the more resplendent his words became. He had no idea why.

Cheever, meanwhile, was enraptured with the invaluable information he was gathering. Until now anthro-entomologists had believed what Sledge was calling death orgies were either tribal wars or culling. This was also the first anyone had heard of the Opifex. Unfortunately, the slaw locust was often too weak from the lack of interrogation to provide further details. Cheever approached Director Hoot once again with his findings, to ask if he could please stop incapacitating his test subject for no *weason*.

"But of course there is a *weason*, Doctor. His physical distress helps foster the emotional bond with Private Anglewood which your *wesearch* relies upon. So, if anything, you should be thanking us. In fact, to optimize the results of your study, I suggest we start asking Private Anglewood no questions too."

Cheever considered this for a moment.

"No," he decided. "As it is, we scarcely have to work for the information we're gathering. This bug is an absolute narcissist, he can't wait to show off what he knows. The only limit to the intelligence we're receiving is the debilitation he receives from your torture techniques."

"We don't use that word, Lieutenant. Listen, your study is fascinating—I enjoy fairy tales as much as anyone—but we have the safety of the Hominid Alliance to consider, so don't be resentful. In fact, why don't you join us in three days when we finally pull its wings off? The colonel and his staff will be in attendance. And there'll be punch!"

"I will not participate in this . . . *bawbawism*!"

Director Hoot sighed. "In all fairness, Doctor Lieutenant, it is I who ought to be complaining to you. Your so-called subject is becoming hostile. Yesterday while we were testing its resilience against exoskeletal torsion fractures, it sang nonstop the entire session."

Cheever stomped his boot in frustration. "You see?" he cried. "Even unprompted, he's surrendering information about unstudied killbug cultural phenomena. Confinement rituals, death orgies!"

"No," said the Director. "That at least would have been pleasurable. About Beta's fourth moon. Your people's twisted water sports! For five hours. One of our inquisitors is still in trauma care."

Cheever asked to see the footage from the sessions. The Director replied the footage had been destroyed and furthermore never existed. But when Cheever said he just wanted to watch the bastard writhe a bit, he was shown into a viewing room and served punch.

Even if killbugs don't feel fear, they are still susceptible to torture because the extreme stimulation can overload their neural relays. To keep their minds from breaking, they must find a way to maintain mental autonomy from their tormentors. Sledge's approach was to visualize his interaction with the Psi Ward as a frolicking match and call the play-by-play.

To understand the video, Cheever had to remember that killbugs are both amused and bewildered by the human concept of "points," the assignment of numerical values to what can be neither counted nor measured. For instance, it made no sense to Sledge that a splashmo should be worth two and a half ripplers. So Sledge enthusiastically assigned point values to everything his captors did, from the trivial and commonplace to the agonizing and deadly.

"Here come the friendlies for the play match!" he sang. "Hollowfoot and Fatnose, your friendly matchers! Hurray them, watching ones! Flatulence, let the frolicks begin! Fatnose removes keys from hipsack. Cleanly done, Fatnose, six points. Now the unlock . . . Unlocked! Concerning that! Alert now, Fatnose crossing the floor . . . Crosses! Niiiice footwork by Fatnose. You witness it! Applies cranial pressure . . . Sob the pain. Niiiice pressure, Fatnose, again! Wavemash, power score! A done the master movement, yes!

"Ooh, here come footsie for follow-up . . . Shanked it! Blame! Bad footsie, funny footsie for Hollowfoot. Six points anyway! Try again, Hollowfoot. Cry the god mother ouch the pain. What a scored on Sledge, far-shining splashmo! The eyes do not believe it! The crowd fartleslurps for Hollowfoot! Good fecund whore the Hollowfoot mother, may she whore out many yet like Hollowfoot!

"Wait, attentive witness! Fatnose ziggies open the burn bag, mighty burnies inside! Nicely ziggied, Fatnose, thirty points. Burny sticks burning now—there's some hot burny. O wicked rippler! Bloody anus eating, what a burning. Well burnt by Fatnose!

"Toot toot. Uh oh! Toots from the striper! Well tooted,

striper, twelve points for tooting. Will the striper stand the burny? Stripers huddle, talk a mumble. Well mumbled, stripers, forty-eight points for good mumbly. Silence, ahush the eat hole, make moments . . . Stripers make it stand! Burny stands! Well stood, stripers! Seventy-two points to Fatnose! And twelve points to the stripers for standing it!"

Over time, however, the distress of questions not asked by the Psi Ward technicians made Sledge increasingly disoriented. Yet in his more lucid moments, he would confess to Peter that sometimes he daydreamed of the frolic, his six buggy legs replaced by four limbs better suited for scoring squeal-walls and fish-spits.

Nauseating, I know. Still, it meant something that a killbug had buried its violent nature enough to daydream, however imprecisely, of a carefree youth on Beta. Cheever didn't know how much of this personality displacement was due to Anglewood's influence and how much to extensive mutilation, searing agony, and approaching death, but it'd be lunacy not to explore it further. For the fourth time, Cheever asked Director Hoot to hand over Sledge for study.

"Out of the question," the Director said. "By now, the lack of interrogation has reduced the slaw locust to an unrecognizable mess. As it is, the death blow will barely get a twitch out of him. If we don't kill him now, there won't be any point to it at all."

"The point of the Psi Ward isn't to watch them suffer. It's to obtain information!"

"Let's not mince words, Dr. Waldorf. Suffering and information amount to the same thing, don't they?"

"What? For whom?"

"Oh, and we plan to execute Anglewood too, while we're up."

Cheever was flabbergasted. "For what, cowardice? While four-fifths of his company was being blown to bits around him, Pete Anglewood stood atop a hill and sang, pitch perfect. With his eyes closed! Say what you want about the man, but he's no coward."

"All right, Doctor. You may have 'justice' on your side. But think about the Psi Ward boys for once, would you? It's been ages since they got to execute anyone, it's not fair to them. Besides," the Director added, "Private Anglewood has been subjected to weeks of subversive reprogramming by a hostile agent. Who knows what threat he now represents? No less than a four-month period of not being asked questions would be required to determine if it was safe to return him to the line."

"Safe for what?" demanded Cheever. "Between facing execution on trumped-up charges and being left to sit in darkness listening to Sledge romanticize death orgies for weeks on end, Anglewood wants to murder everything in sight. He can't wait to run out and bathe his limbs in the blood of the enemy and raw-eat their flesh. I have to remind him how dangerous bug goo is to consume."

"Is it really?"

"Not if you don't mind boiling out your innards and shitting blood."

"Huh. That is something. I'll keep that in mind for future investigations. Anyways, I have already signed the papers for Private Anglewood's execution tomorrow. I could rescind the order, but you would not believe the bureaucracy involved. No man's life is worth that kind of hassle."

You all remember how this ended. On that last night, for two poets disparate in both appearance and ideology, the fraternity of their art proved stronger than the war between them. They sat up awaiting their deaths together, huddled close in tears, fury, and laughter, exchanging embraces, mingling their blood.

When the military police came at dawn to cart them off

to their fates, the night watchman whispered, "Look out, they're planning something in there."

As the key turned in the lock, Sledge and Anglewood stood side by side, facing the door in perfect serenity. Light entered the cell, stretching across the floor to where it lay at Anglewood's feet.

"Welcome, gentlemen," he said from the darkness. "From the way you clutch your weapons, it appears you're expecting an act of poetry. On the contrary, I'd like to speak plainly on behalf of myself and this killbug. Today, so close to the end, we have no flowery speech or obscure allusions. We simply wish to be understood. So please indulge a few words. I'll be brief."

The MPs, who had latrine duty after escorting these two to the firing wall, nodded to Anglewood to continue. The mound of pulled pork beside him drew itself up painfully to vouch for his words.

"This killbug you condemn to death for fighting for his kind; me, you will execute for not fighting vigorously enough. Whatever may have brought us two, born worlds apart, to die here together today is larger than any of us. We did not create the forces which rule our fates, yet at this hour our lives are forfeit to them. We could make peace with this, we might decry it as unfair, but what can we *do* about it?

"The galaxy is not a place any single person can hope to shape. In the crush of events, it seems a miracle to have existed at all. Even before this battle to extinction between hominids and killbugs, the galaxy often appeared harsh, even evil. What, then, can we hope for with our tiny flicker of existence, our brief gasp of individuality? This is a question no Psi Ward technician has ever thought to ask.

"Yet this slaw locust and I would like to assert that *art remains an answer*. We believe that in even the most unsympathetic galaxy, it is still worthwhile to show the truth—not merely an oppressor's narrative, or even the reproaches of the subjugated, but the galaxy complete in all its brutal color and breathtaking wonder, portrayed with vigor and an attention to detail that neither sugarcoats nor falls prey to cynicism, chained to no ideology, slave to no dogma—born in experience, buoyed up by beauty—an art that reveals the world.

"Why does art matter? Because by casting light into the rare corners of our existence where truth and beauty meet, it suffuses the galaxy with love, love which though it may lack the power to rectify, retains the power to *redeem*.

"This slaw locust and I were poets. I sang of the

frolicking matches of the Betan youth, Sledge of the death orgies of the killbugs. Although our subject matter was different, our approach was similar. The traditions toward which we aimed our art were imperfect—even deeply flawed—but I humbly submit we have both seen directly to the joy of these things. Each of us believes in the power of poetry. It memorializes with love, it transfigures through love, poetry *is* love.

"For centuries now, people have complained poetry is obsolete, that poetry is *terrible*. And while it's true that poetry *as language* has been sick, *as love* it continues to flourish both on the human worlds and in killbug space. As this slaw locust and I bear witness today, poetry thrives *as love*, if not in words then in action. For whatsoever is done in joy or wonder, whatever gives dimension both to the moment at hand and to the static eternity we call time, that too is poetry, that too is love.

"I am Peter Festoon Anglewood, Betan born. This slaw locust whom you call Sledge, bears a name I am not endowed to pronounce. We stand here before you today facing execution, threatening to *commit poetry* against you one last time. Well then, this is the kind of poetry with which we have armed ourselves: one last gesture of truth illuminating one last corner of beauty, spoken without words but louder than the combined roar of all your atom scramblers. We lose our lives today, but you take nothing from us, because through love in action, we now belong to eternity. Watch now!"

The MPs reached for their holsters, but it was too late. With a movement too slight to notice, Anglewood raised a concealed weapon and shot Sledge through the face. The cranial plate exploded, and the bits fluttered down like confetti. Rolling his eyes up into his head, Anglewood fell hard onto his knees and feasted orgiastically on Sledge's half roasted brains.

Turns out all those nights Sledge had spent writhing, too incapacitated to speak, Anglewood had been constructing a boson refibrucator out of his bedsprings. By sapping energy from Cheever's translation equipment, he'd stored up enough power to fire a single blast. Apparently, in addition to being shitty at poetry, Anglewood was an unparalleled genius at harnessing the power of elementary particles. Who knew?

Anyway, if you watch the surveillance video of that night (hey, I like punch), Anglewood assures Sledge that before sunup they would breathe life together into their poetry one last time. The sad thing is, if you read the transcription, it's obvious Sledge thought Pete was promising to take him swimming, to teach him the breaststroke and how to score splashmos while making high-pitched squeals in celebration of sublunar life.

"Oh, how I great distance to wear a onesie and steal other larvae onesies, to hamtie the jiggly ones with their own onesies and stain them with my in-mes. How I eat and drink to lay my skin-shell in the soak and have lazy feeling enter the airholes, to strike hand-foots on the bang-skins and burn the plants and make harmonic mouth noises. Much I remember-hurt to paint the bodies colors then appreciate the colors and not see the UV colors. 'Hey, you one,' I say to the jiggly, 'do you not the UV on me?' 'Yes,' says the jiggly, hiccupping, 'I do not see it very well.' 'Fifty-four points for not seeing! Come you, I to not slaughter you now!' 'Yes, let's quick to the not slaughtering! I make the la la's with my eat-hole! La la. Now you.' 'La la la.' 'By gore, good la, Charlie! Eighty-four points! Triple splashmo!' Belabored breath. Ah, such edible hallucinations."

Well, it's for the best Anglewood shot him. Nothing more loathsome in the Opifex's wide universe than a killbug gone granola.

The strange twist. Although it's punishable by death to execute a prisoner without permission, by committing this

162

crime Anglewood staved off his own execution. Sledge's death, being the first time Anglewood had shot anything, demonstrated he'd finally adopted the military mindset and pledged himself to hominid objectives. The court martial interpreted this murder as a rejection of everything with which the locust had tried to indoctrinate him—whereas if you had more than half a head (unlike poor Sledge), you'd realize Sledge's conversion of Anglewood had been almost total. After all, it was the romance of the death orgy which had inspired him to violence: among Sledge's people it was a gesture of love and respect.

Right. Well, all for naught, because yesterday peedlebugs ate Anglewood.

I'm hungry too, come to mention it. What do you say we leave this here and head to dinner? Oh Pete, you stupid lovely fuck, whatever did they do to you? From the sublunar shores of Beta's fourth moon, to the dirty prisons of Cayenne Rock, to every shithole outpost in the galaxy, you were always the man you were born to be. Nobody could ever destroy what was beautiful in you. You *were* love, in your own twisted way. Shit, Pete. Rest in peace. We'll miss you. Ad saecu sec. Amen.

THE DEATH OF CHEEVER WALDORF

WHAT A TRAUMA WATCHING CHEEVER hatch yesterday. Larvae slithered out his ear, like baby Gargantuas—one after another, *plop*, right into his gruel.

"How'd they get so big?" he asked quietly, holding up a grub between his fingers. "Brain tissue, I suppose."

As if in confirmation, he keeled over. Dead before his face hit the porridge. The autopsy showed—what are we calling autopsy these days? Gilbert Rasher rattling his shitpick 'round inside his skull—showed about only a quarter of his gray matter remained when the gristlebugs decided to abandon ship. A testament that he lasted so long.

Even when we were kids, Cheever Waldorf had brains to spare. If a gristly had laid an egg or two in that bulbous head back then, it'd have done him a favor. Cheever's intellect was so adept at cataloging all variables and contingencies, he could never see anything with certainty. Which explains the savage determination of his final days: his skull had become an echo chamber. But he died like a Betan warrior: shooting and stabbing everything in sight until nothing was left alive to twitch.

Prior to that, he'd fought with a forked soul. Had one or two cards fallen differently, he might've sided with the enemy. Yes, Cheever had buggist sympathies. As our embedded anthro-entomologist, it was his job to understand their motives and objectives—and they appealed to him. Efficiency is next to godliness for a man like Cheever; he preferred the simple elegance of the bug's war strategy over the convoluted plots and machinations of men.

But one day his warrior instinct suddenly switched on, converting him wholesale to the cause of human civilization over insect. The entire hive empire became for him one more *delenda est*, to be wiped out without hesitancy or conscience. What had gotten into him? Turns out a couple dozen gristly eggs, relieving him of the burden of intellect.

Cheever was not here to fight but to study. As a child,

he wanted to be a galaxy-class entomologist. While we were gently parting the limpid pools (et cetera ad nauseum), he spent his youth marveling at the krain-gliders as they darted frictionlessly across the rag scum atop the water. He tagged their itty-bitty buggy footsies to monitor their resin gathering behaviors and digitally analyze their pathways.

"No society," he told us then, "is as structured, as perfect, as beautiful as the hive."

We were eight years old when hominid linguists made their monumental breakthrough: the killbugs, with their complex species-caste structures, were organized by relays based primarily on, yes, language! The stumbling block to this discovery had been that their verbal communication was not fundamentally oral. A killbug with its innumerable aeration holes produced a veritable fugue of sounds, many—but not all!—of which were phonemically significant. It had been a headache to sort out which were which, but the linguists determined, not without glee, that killbugs literally talk out of their ass.

It was one of the great intellectual triumphs of our age when that cacophony of static, wheezepops, and fartwhistles was reduced to discrete lexographic items, then finally coherent insectoid ideas.

Bug-speak has a dizzying number of inflections,

necessary since the syntax is non-linear: the gases utilized for locution, not limited to exhaled breath, are synthesized at different rates by various organic processes and cannot be expelled before they become available. (Which means shooting a killbug in the liver might cause it to develop a speech impediment. Funny, that.) While maddening to decipher, the countless noun cases provide a finer precision of language, free of much of the ambiguity in human speech. This permits the bugs—the smart ones anyway—a greater clarity in which to discuss mathematics, philosophy, social engineering, and military strategy.

I'm not sure eight-year-old Cheever understood what a phoneme was (or maybe he did), but that breakthrough sparked a lifelong interest in killbugs. The more he learned, the more he admired them. Unlike the intelligent hominids of the galaxy, the myriad species of killbugs have successfully integrated into one seamless interworld social structure—a voluntary empire. Just as cells in the body do not fight over which are neurons or which will form muscle tissue, lungs, or the liver, killbug rulers, laborers, and technicians all arrive at their place in society of their own accord.

How the killbugs attained this elegant and robust order is yet unclear to anthro-entomologists. Some assert the bugs evolved a genetic disposition toward selfless cooperation. This would mean their society was effectively incorruptible. Yet Cheever held out hope their pan-galactic union was orchestrated through the creativity and will of individuals. If so, it might provide a template for hominids to study and imitate. For Cheever, the killbugs represented the possibility of human perfection.

Listen. Insects: either you love 'em or you find 'em revolting. They are the life form most alien to us, the least human. Free of pride and charity and most other human qualities, they do not waste conspicuously. They're not swayed by iconography or ideology. They put no value on beauty. They never recoil at filth, death bears no solemnity for them. Devoid of emotion, they understand neither pity nor revenge. For us, they are monsters, but to Cheever, they represented the ideal. Their values offered a counterbalance to every deficiency in human life, especially his own.

Cheever's parents were political agitators. His mother especially pushed for the gradual dismantling of the ragnarite industry. It poisoned the water, created a safety hazard for millions of workers, exploited the outer worlds, fomented political tension between Beta and Earth, and made us entirely reliant on a resource which in a few centuries would be completely exhausted. She was a crackpot, of course. Beta produces only two things, ragnarite and electric storms, what other choice did we have?

The Waldorfs exposed their son to a broad spectrum of ideas. They encouraged him to challenge everything and to identify the virtues and flaws of every argument and counterargument. No wonder he was a self-loathing prick. This upbringing failed to provide Cheever with any direction while denying him any obvious path for expressing his individuality. The more clearly he saw through turns of rhetoric, the more he perceived only chaos in the world around him.

Cheever despised his parents for the anxiety and doubt they created in him. Even so, he could not tolerate hearing them criticized in public. As a teenager, this proved an irresolvable crisis.

Insects appealed to him because a bug's life possessed no complex political philosophy. An insect's work was an end in itself, bearing no burden of identity. A bug never had to choose between its friends and an ideology, or determine if the viewpoint of its adversaries had any merit. Because he could not bear standing out from others, Cheever esteemed the bugs more highly, which naturally made him a greater standout. He was conspicuously his own worst enemy.

You had to wonder if he felt so isolated, how come he never joined the rest of us at the frolic in the sublunar pools on Beta's fourth moon? I've no idea if Cheever even knew how to swim! (Although if he did, I'm sure it would have been without peer.)

Of all you bastards I had the misfortune to grow up with, Cheever Waldorf was the only one I hated. The only one I never had cause to. So many things came so readily to that brilliant head of his, sometimes he'd dumb things down just so he wouldn't upset us. That was a mistake. Nothing's worse than a magnanimous know-it-all. If he'd really had any brains, he would have made *us* feel inadequate before we had a chance to do it to him. Remember the way he'd check over his midterms seven times just to not turn them in an hour before everyone else? Or that polite way he'd correct the teacher's math mistakes when no one was looking? If there really was something he couldn't do, then we persecuted him. In the end, he spent all his time trying to tiptoe the line between our hatred and his humiliation. I ought to have felt sorry him, but that only made me detest him more.

Cheever could speak every language on Beta. Six! (Even

Earth had only four in her last days!) It was pathetic watching him try to convince us that his Hamline was "kinda rusty," even though the scores on his oral examination had just gotten him appointed junior district ambassador to Hamline.

Cheever had so much brains, nobody could figure out how to use him—except for those brainless tasks which people with no brains make up to keep busy the people with too much brains. Like junior district ambassador to Hamline. It's very simple process, you just go up to the brainy one and say, "mm, excuse me but, we need you to . . ." then follow up with something that would never, ever need to be done. Then Cheever did it. Of course, he knew it was a waste of time, but he wanted too much to be liked.

So why were we surprised Cheever had buggist sympathies? He admired a society where those who can pile shit are shitpilers, those with real talent do useful stuff, and worthless fuck-ups are junior district ambassadors.

Hey, remember when we spent three weeks squatting in a bog outside Strikepost Seedlebridge harpooning dugbugs to keep them from harvesting amberthin, even though nobody knew yet what amberthin was for? In the evenings we'd chew up the amberthin and spit it on Cheever. Months later, we found out amberthin's only use was for the bugs to spray it on the bugs they didn't like. God damn, that was funny!

Oh, and then we learned that extended exposure to amberthin causes topical paralysis and Cheever could no longer feel his face. That was funny too!

As a teenager, he dreamed of studying the bugs and their wondrous social organism up close. When us boys used to brag how one day we'd smear them all, every hideous, filth-covered, barbaric one of 'em, Cheever got defensive. He said the bugs were so superior to us, the senseless destruction of one society by another wasn't even coherent to them. In fact, just the idea of action so counterproductive would embarrass them, if they were capable of emotions as counterproductive as embarrassment.

Then the killbugs ashed the Earth. Whoops.

Cheever began to drink.

Well, the war was lucky for his career. It used to be impossible to get funding for research stations on rocks in bug space, but the moment black smoke choked off all life on Earth, the field of anthro-entomology suddenly had strategic value.

The bump in the defense budget also meant military outposts could now protect research facilities. This gave someone a brilliant idea: integrate the researchers with the combat troops. Hey, scientists! While you're out waving your digi-analysis rods, take a smuon/squark rifle with you. You finished studying a bug? Good, put a bullet in him. Hey, why not be a *physical* anthro-entomologist? Examine which way their cerebral nodes splatter when you shoot them.

Scientists despaired when they heard the brass's vision of a harmonious blend of war and research. "Wesearch" they started calling it. Part nerd humor, part genuine protest. But even with the conflict of interest, Cheever was eager to seize this opportunity, believing the study of killbugs stood at a new frontier.

The chief grievance against the bugs had always been that their society was soulless and entirely devoid of culture. But Cheever and Anglewood discovered this was incorrect, that the killbugs have almost unlimited stores of oral history and verse. Plus, they had so many unexplained group behaviors: who knew what other cultural forms the bugs were practicing right under our noses? Some could be theater. Some could be opera! Or art forms humans never invented because we lack the collective consciousness the insects seem to possess.

It's believed that no hominid mind will ever grasp

killbug music without the aid of technology. Killbug ears can distinguish, pitch perfect, a staggering thirty-six semitones, not to mention a bewildering number of keys and modes. The majority of songs cataloged so far are marches that keep swarms of killbugs moving in unison. Every line of verse has exactly six syllables, each corresponding to the movement of one leg or a combination of legs. Direction also appears to be encoded, but since it varies from rock to rock, the motion may be relative to the magnetic poles. Their activity is also coordinated in space, so it's presumed the bugs possess subsonic songs as well, but like all their extra-atmospheric communication, it is poorly understood. The researcher under whom Cheever studied for his doctoral thesis had investigated interstellar killbug transmissions extensively. After a decade, he concluded that they accomplish it through a process he called "black magic."

Cheever transcribed four hundred songs from the slaw locust Sledge, performed between ask-no-questions sessions on Cayenne Rock. Every damn one of them is about killing stuff or stuff dying, all in brutal disgusting ways. This sampling allowed Cheever to identify roughly one hundred eighty words for killing things and at least one hundred thirty words for states of being dead. I've cribbed a partial list of them from Cheever's notes for your enjoyment. Ahem:

There's dead, newly dead, messily dead, honorably dead, dead long enough to stink, dead and remembered, dead and forgotten, dead and belonging to the ages (this supposes complete decomposition), dead and eaten, holy dead, dishonored dead, dead by puncture, dead by live burial, dead by burning, starved to death, missing and presumed dead, atomized dead, killed so dead your grandchildren feel it, dead but tasty looking, dead due to atmospheric conditions, dead with living progeny, dead with progeny smeared, decapitated and dead (not redundant for some bugs), dead and floating in space, having died alone, dead among multitudes, drowned, suffocated, bled to death, and finally something Cheever whimsically called "Elvis dead."

The word for dead, plain old, is literally "legs up."

The stunning thing about these poems is that the attitude toward death, whether of friend or foe, is invariably *ecstatic!* Death—even untimely death—*can't come quick enough!*

A common way of filling out a short poetic line is the disyllabic "praise God," or as Cheever kept insisting, "Praise the Opifex." This is a very old word meaning "work-doer," which in ancient Earth days referred to the supernatural being who built the cosmos with his own two hands. Judging by how the name is invoked, the Opifex's only pleasure is in the obliteration of everything in sight. This Opifex is somehow both immortal *and* dead (dishonored). Plus, the Queen "shits" him. The Queen shits God? "Emerges from the waste hole" is the literal translation. For killbugs, shit has sacred connotations, but this still seems a theological perplexity.

Some anthro-entomologists question if the Hive Queen is even real. She would be the only organism in the galaxy capable of spawning species other than her own. Her features are never described. Even the bugs whom the Psi Ward has not asked questions the most vigorously do not seem to know in which part of the galaxy she resides. Nevertheless, the Queen is called the Author of All Song. This honorary title suggests something like Commander-in-Chief, since music is part of all coordinated death making, whether in war or routine culling.

While we were still squashing dugbugs at Strikepost Seedlebridge to test Cheever's wild hypothesis about the role of amberthin in nymph conditioning (he believed it was to accelerate adrenal development), the Anthro-Entomological Institute completed its first analysis of the bug lore Cheever had collected with Anglewood on Cayenne Rock.

From a close study of the poems' vocabulary, the report determined that the Opifex—whom the first Queen dutifully minces and devours following the creation of the cosmos—this peculiar creator god is described as having not insect but hominid anatomy! No shit. Their god is a man! What's more, the sacred imperative to rend and consume the Opifex's body is understood also to apply to the sentient beings created in his image, i.e. people! In other words, this unending war the killbugs wage against hominids is conducted as an act of piety—*to us!*

That's when Cheever began to really drink.

I can't say I blame him. The killbug model for eliminating intra-species struggle had been to redirect the impulse to violence outward in an unending concerted act of murder/suicide. For humanity, it now appeared that perpetuating its current condition—century after century of infighting, misery, and ruin due to our unquenchable thirst for commodity and status—represented the best hope for the future. What was a defeated ideologue like Cheever to do but drink?

Sodden as he was, he did not give up completely. Cheever believed death-worship, as described in the literature, was preposterous, even for creatures as alien and vicious as killbugs. Undoubtedly, the social function of these poems was misunderstood, and further study would alleviate the confusion. But for now, the evidence suggested cooperation with the killbugs would be antithetical to every human instinct. The burden fell on Cheever to show how any policy but total war made sense.

In the end, he found what he was looking for. Although if he knew the price the bugs would make him pay for it, he might have declined.

From here on, the story gets tricky. A serviceman could be hanged just for knowing of the existence of the classified material I'm going to talk about. But Cheever spilled everything months ago. How could anyone someone so consistently shitfaced protect secrets for any length of time?

Hammered on bwain damage, Cheever claimed the true reason we are on Thisone has nothing to do with mantis fighters. Our mission was a cover for his clandestine wesearch operation. Not even Major Croop had been briefed on the particulars before our deployment. "I'm gathering intelligence invaluable for the development of successful military strategy." Sure you are, Doc. You're covered in shit like the rest of us, and you can barely stand, let alone operate that computer of yours.

Cheever had prerogative to ignore protocols and nullify orders at his discretion, so long as it didn't jeopardize the task force. Between him and the Major, this created a tension, frequently exacerbated by Cheever's belligerence and not-so-secret drinking. (Just because a pill could nullify the motor effects of alcohol shortly before a sloop run didn't make the ravages on his body any less visible.)

After a protracted fit of curses and weeping, Cheever divulged he was looking for a special bug called the Queen's Consort. A few dozen lines among the hundreds of thousands recited by Sledge on Cayenne Rock suggested that the Consort resides, or at least originates, in this corner of the galaxy. There is no data on what this Consort looks like, how big, or what color he is, but Cheever conjectured he wouldn't look like any killbug we'd ever seen. Most likely, he would be large since the Queen is rumored to lay sizable eggs, but it doesn't necessarily follow. Of course, the question remains why the Queen, unlike most killbug egg-layers, would have only one Consort, leading Cheever to wonder if the Consort's chief function was something other than reproduction.

Since the Consort presumably has some contact with the Queen, identifying him might be the first step to locating her. Of course, the brass didn't put a ton of faith in the ravings of a half-dead slaw locust, but the easiest way to keep Cheever from making a ruckus with his findings was to give him a promotion, dump a security clearance on him, and grant him a free hand to do whatever the hell he wanted in the silent space beyond the frontier. Who knew? He might find something. If he's killed, recover his notes. Destroy them if they are inconvenient. Everyone wins.

Except, of course, the sorry bastards in his military escort. You know, us.

Well, Roger Kean didn't come here for science. He was invested in the success of the mantis mission: dismantle the factories, show his grit in the face of terrifying foes, become the shining example of courage and honor for young men throughout the Alliance. Get off this damn rock alive and take his rightful place among the hominid leadership.

But Doctor Cheever Waldorf cared about none of that. In fact, he preferred if we didn't kill any mantes on the sloop runs.

Although the bugs' tactical movements are mandated by their combat music, it's known that a V.I.B. such as the

181

Consort will emit a subsonic static that interferes with the way the killbugs respond to their march orders. This modification varies between species: some become more aggressive, some hold back and defend, others pile the filth faster, etc. etc. Increased proximity with the leadership bug magnifies the effect, and it also strengthens with prolonged exposure. The key to locating the source of the Consort's interference was to tag subjects and collect precise measurements on the mantes' combat movement over time. Unfortunately, Cheever complained, every time we killed one of the tagged fighters, we nullified another heap of his meticulously gathered data. "The manifest idiocy of wesearch!" he cried.

Instead of smearing the bugs, Cheever wanted us to trigger the war-singer's hive-defense march, then provide cover while he collected data on the tagged fighters' movements. For most of us, that was no problem. We were content just to finish the day with our cocks on.

But Roger Kean was determined to see the factory dismantled.

Stand the two men toe-to-toe before public opinion: Cheever's intellect versus Roger Kean's charisma. Poor Cheever.

Roger Kean publicly accused him of trying to protect

the mantes. Of course, he was trying to protect them! He had fought his whole life for an opportunity to study the culture and civilization of the killbugs, and now he was under orders to commit genocide against them. It was too much to ask of anyone.

". . . and endangering the lives of our men!" cried Roger Kean.

To be fair, why shouldn't he? Throughout his life, Cheever had committed no greater offense than wanting to use his considerable intellect for our benefit, and we always punished him for it. Was it so strange he now found something more important than protecting the lives of the people who had persecuted him?

Roger Kean asked us to imagine the next time we faced a mantis fighter bearing down on us: left scythe, right scythe, face and fuckknob! Did we really believe the study of something yet unseen and possibly nonexistent was vastly more important than our own safety? Don't forget, Roger Kean reminded us, Cheever Waldorf is the same man who involved us in that fiasco with the dugbugs and the amberthin.

Everything Roger Kean said about Cheever had a ring of truth, which was what upset him so much. Yes, Cheever *was* committing treason here, but a treason against himself:

he had prepared tirelessly for years to study the thing he loved, and now that the opportunity arose, he was helping to destroy it.

Roger Kean demanded Cheever be stripped of his wesearch prerogatives for the sake of the mission, and over time he coaxed more and more of us over to his point of view. With Cheever's drunken surliness, we didn't need much convincing.

But it's Major Croop who gives the orders. After six months on Thisone, Cheever approached the Major with data that showed the way the mantes were dejunking us was changing over time, suggesting the presence of a V.I.B. Moreover, using some frightfully complex mathematics, Cheever reverse engineered the static pattern emitted by the V.I.B. and show it did not fall within the range of any killbug on record. We were confronting an entirely new leadership caste *in the immediate vicinity of the camp*. With continued analysis, he could pinpoint its position exactly.

. . . Although, he confessed, the data were problematic: the subsonic effect of the mysterious killbug sometimes varied so violently, it didn't seem to be just moving around but appearing and disappearing at will.

Cheever never knew when to shut up.

But he pressed on with his case. The evidence he presented consisted of textual criticism of poems written in an almost incomprehensible killbug language and some high order mathematics I doubt half the eggheads on Akadademo could understand. In effect, it boiled down to Cheever trying to inspire faith in the Major that Cheever had faith in himself. You know as well as I that Cheever had been plagued with self-doubt his whole life. He left the meeting visibly upset, convinced the Major would side with Roger Kean and give the order to destroy a lifetime of his work.

So no one was more surprised than Cheever when Major Croop announced our objectives had changed. We were no longer here to dismantle mantis factories, but to provide combat cover for Captain Waldorf's search for a possible V.I.B. on this rock.

Croop defended his decision saying, "In my estimation, the best chance for ultimate human victory is to execute a decapitation strike against the killbug leadership. To make such a strike possible, the Sons of Beta will proudly bear any burden, for the glory of the homeworld and the salvation of humankind.

"I have known Captain Waldorf since he was old enough to walk. His parents have always taught him to act with honor and integrity, and I have never known him to do otherwise. I have spoken with the Captain in private and asked him to evaluate for me on his honor, with the lives of his comrades at stake, the credibility of information he has shown me. He has fully convinced me that the possibility of such a discovery is worth the risk entailed. Therefore, in light of his advisement, you are to assume a defensive footing during the mantis counter assaults. Your fire will only discourage their attack, you will not force them into the open for the purpose of eliminating them."

In essence, Croop was forsaking our hard-fought mission for the sake of Cheever's wesearch, deferring to the captain's judgment despite the months of ill-feeling between them, despite mounting pressure from Roger Kean to adopt more aggressive tactics.

Well, as far as I know, a leadership bug is already more likely to sit down at mess for biscuits than we are to dismantle a killbug factory, so I understand the Major's point of view. But his decision still surprised me. I wouldn't have the courage to order any of you, Rampage of Beta, not to put down a mantis when you had the opportunity. It was touching to see Cheever finally vindicated.

But then disaster. Cheever had noticed his data growing more erratic, but he didn't grasp the cause until he found one mantis fighter wearing *three* of his tags. The mantes were now regarding the silicon wafers Cheever had embedded in their body armor as good luck charms, since it made them much less likely to draw fire. They gambled for them between sloop runs, and the loser would saw out the section of plating and patch it directly onto the dorsal ridge of whoever had beat him at draughts, or whatever killbugs play.

All his data were now completely useless. Cheever disappeared for days in a blind rage. When he regained his senses, he reported to the Major what he had discovered, swallowing his pride in front of Roger Kean.

What did pride matter? Now even the killbugs had betrayed him. They worshiped death in all its forms, so what were they doing gambling for charms? This detail—which ought to have encouraged him, since it suggested the killbugs didn't really possess the bleak worldview their poetry presented—only upset him more, since it had destroyed months of labor, performed under threat of hideous mutilation and professional humiliation.

So, Cheever gave up on the bugs. He stood in front of the mirror and stained his face with war paint: on each cheek two eyes with enormous blue irises. He made himself a six-eyed monster infiltrating the hive to slaughter everyone—men, women, children—to burn the crèches, smash the eggs, skewer the living, and grind the corpses beneath his heel.

He showed up for morning sloop with his smuon/squark blaster, iced out on nerve calmant for the DTs. He was done with science, he said, he'd come to fight.

"Kill 'em! Smoke 'em and smear 'em!"

We laughed and raised an ironic cheer.

But he was first into the sloop that morning. Forgot his sludge-flow redirector, so he nearly drowned leading the charge. No steady hand either, but he recalibrated his targeter to compensate for the shakes. Like a gray ghost among our ranks, he shouted orders—a captain after all— his voice echoing up and down the tunnels, alerting the entire fuckhill to our presence. I thought Cheever had simply decided to die that day: it wouldn't be the first time we've seen a death wish expressed as blood lust.

When Cheever went down under the pile, I murmured an ad saecu sec for him. It was nearly a minute before I realized he was still under there, fighting off the mantes.

After we dragged him out by his heels, we had to restrain him from diving back in.

"Weddy to wesearch," he kept screaming. "Widdle wesearch wid my wifle. Weddy or not, the wath of the human wace. Waze and wapine, weap the pwice of twechewy, you tweasonous wogues!"

He didn't so much cut a swath as get lucky not to be killed. I guess you can't just show up one day and pull down worlds from the foundations. But what a show!

Then gristle larvae ate his brains out. As they emptied his head, Cheever became, nibble by nibble, mouthful by mouthful, well . . . human. Frankly, I believe he was happy in the end. The deadly parasites helped him kill without conflict. For once in his life, he enjoyed unity of thought, purity of will.

God damn it all! Men or insects. This or that. Must our choices always be so binary, between two outlooks so equally blind? Choose between them or face scorn, ostracism, isolation. To not abandon yourself to the insanity of partisanship means to give yourself over to loneliness. That is the price of mind.

Yet in the end, I feel sorry for Cheever, even in his happiness. That internal conflict was what was beautiful about him. Suffering was the soul he possessed. Some people have it killed in them by catastrophe, some poisoned by ideology. Cheever had his soul eaten out of his skull. Oh well.

My friend, I cannot wish back what they took from you, nor can I bear the thought of you without it. Across the breadth of eternity, may you find peace. In the stillness of time may you be free of questions: want not, seek not, fear not. Ad saeculum saeculorum.

THE DEATH OF GILBERT RASHER

GILBERT RASHER SWORE THAT he would never die.

I almost declined to speak today, not because I didn't want to attend his funeral—I'd never refuse the pleasure—but because I'm afraid to stand so close to his corpse. Even now, he's got that vacant look on his face, like a mummy about to get up any moment and strangle us. Because he must be shamming. He told us time and again he had a charm on his life that would protect him till Doomsday. I never believed anything Rasher said, but for some reason, I believed that.

Well, there's Rasher killed, and all goddamn creation still here.

I'm glad to see we're burying that knife with him. Did someone put it in his hand, or did it get there on its own?

He used to lick that thing clean for hours, both sides, over and over, like a tooth or claw. The worst was when he licked it *at* somebody—you'd better watch him when he did. Take your eye off him for an instant, you were liable to feel its tip under one of your ribs. An almost imploring look in his eye: Mother, may I? Baby, please?

Did Rasher want to kill us? Of course he did. He *said* he wanted to kill us, had *plans* to kill us, it just wasn't time. No, not yet. Remember, once we were dead, he still had to live forever. All he could say was, we didn't have to worry about dying quietly in our sleep. We'd all see death coming, that was a promise. Unless he changed his mind.

"I have fifty ways of killing you all," he'd whisper. "Last night I built a death trap for everybody. I assembled it in the dark, just my hands. I examined the mechanism piece by piece, system by system, to make sure it'd work. Check and double check. Then I caressed the trigger. Loooovey! You were all a twitch away from never seeing the sun again. Then I took it apart and hid it. If I wanted to, I could build it again tonight. The pieces are all around you, some of you looking right at them. Sure, break whatever's in front of you, if it'll make you feel better. I have *fifty* of these. I can assemble most of them blindfolded, some with just my teeth."

We never found evidence he was building anything. But he had lies covering lies covering lies, who knew how many layers deep. *Something* was happening here, only Rasher knew what. A secret as bad—or worse!—than death traps for all of us.

Sometimes he smiled sweetly, like he knew how it was going to end—and he couldn't wait.

Weeks ago, I decided the next time I saw Rasher's back, I'd put a bullet in it. I never saw his back again. That's true.

I'm not the only one who wanted to shoot him. The Major said he wanted him shot. But even in the confusion of combat, our weapons all gave Rasher a wide berth. We were afraid to shoot him because Rasher can never die. Some part of me still believes that now.

We've decided to get rid of Rasher's personal belongings in case they include some malicious object we don't recognize, like a bomb or photino cascade. Jettison 'em into space, I say, just to be safe. God knows what contraband he was smuggling around the galaxy in his socks. I can't wait for the last trace of Rasher to be swept away.

Gil's parents were the nicest people I ever knew. He must have been a changeling. People less lovely than the Rashers would have drowned him in the limpid pools of

Beta's fourth moon. Listen, I know this is a eulogy, but if Rasher was here, he'd eat this shit up. He'd laugh so hard, tears would run down his face. "Oh, you guuuuys!" Not that he'd actually feel anything: the fucker could fake it better'n any holograph actor who ever lived.

Even the bugs knew to keep clear of Rasher. He was only an average shot, but he was crafty and he was sick with that knife. Nothing ever died by it without his permission.

Every time Rasher saw a new killbug, he could intuit how it worked, mechanically I mean, just by looking at it. If only he'd been a surgeon instead of a sociopath! With those steady hands and that intimate knowledge of anatomy, he tortured the shit out of things. Remember when he found that "scream switch" on the archer scorpions? He tied two of them up outside the palisade and made them shriek for six days and nights as a "warning" to the rest.

"Physically unable to stop," giggled Rasher, hands over his mouth. "Uncontrollable reflex. Probably hurts a bit too. Hee!"

The other scorpions didn't give a damn—no fear, no pity, them—it was us he was torturing. "Sing, my bea-uuuuties! *Sing!* I even found the pitch control. A little twist here, see? (Sing.) I just set these two screams six semitones apart. One for each leg. Poetry, yes?"

A diminished fifth, a sound so dissonant it's called the devil's interval. He left them like that to die slowly, infusing our dreams with their harrowing screech-whistles. *Lovey*, as Rasher would say.

Once when we were kids, Rasher and I were frolicking on the same scrimmage team when I executed the perfect splashmo/double rippler combo right on our opponents' flank. Rasher swam up for the assist, but I didn't notice. The follow-up squealwall knocked him out into the undertow where I was afraid to go after him. He stayed under a long while. By the time one of the referees fished him out, Rasher needed the water pumped out of his lungs. We were lucky to resuscitate him.

Lucky? I was half in tears.

"Sorry, Gil," I said afterward, "I didn't mean it. Please don't be angry."

At first, I don't think Rasher even understood what had happened. But then his lip started to quiver and he exploded in rage. "I will get you back in six hundred eighty-three days!" he screamed, an inch from my face. "Six. Eight. Three!" thrusting up the wrong number of fingers for each digit.

The outburst seemed theatrical, I forgot about it.

Two years later we were bobbing for guddy and the glass bucket graviton-locked over my head. In my panic, I wrenched up, the whole tank teetering atop my shoulders—must've weighed more than fifty pounds. I ran around kicking up cave dust in my spelunkers, screaming underwater while the little fat-eyed fish swam past my eyes. I smashed the bucket on a low hanging lintel on one of the shaft elevators. It knocked me stupid but the glass didn't break. It took a chisel stroke with a live rag drill to do that. The water poured out as I inhaled my first mouthful.

When I came to, Rasher was balled up in laughter. My nearly drowning amused him. The fact I'd survived was somehow even funnier. Without apparent cause, he apologized. "Soooo sorry, Tim-mey! SAAAARY! Ickle axy-dent! Tee!"

The police decided no foul play was involved. They were embarrassed to admit they couldn't figure out how Gil sabotaged the bucket. But I knew it was him when I checked the log: it was exactly six hundred eighty-three days later.

When the war broke out, Rasher was overjoyed. Just as armies would soon reach out and devour everything they touched, so too would a fog of Rasher spread itself throughout the galaxy. At last, a chance to do anything. *Anything!* Sabotage our own drinking water, the enemy gets the blame. You suspect Rasher but you can't prove it. He's just as sick as the rest of us, or at least he can fake it.

Years ago when we were deployed on Walpurga Rock, Rasher and I were part of a reconnaissance team aiding our mission to relieve Port Benandante under siege from the nimmercrays. High in the nearby cliffs, we were ambushed by crickets, who dragged off the others while Gil and I escaped in the brush. We were about to dial up for an evac when we saw the comm tower go down. Hominid reinforcements had the nimmercrays trapped against the port's outer wall, but we estimated two days for our men to get the cannons inside the fortification and repair the tower.

My first thought was, I'm stranded with this lunatic! Even if I survive the nimmercrays, I'll never escape Rasher. With the two of us alone, only the bugs to mind us, Rasher picked up the scent of total lawlessness in the air, and it had him salivating. That night, I felt his eyes settle upon me, his fingers upon his knife, like he was dividing up my body and deciding which parts to hand over to which sick impulse. I could almost hear some ecstatic corner of his soul crying, "Now, *now* is the time!"

But what, oh what should he do exactly with the opportunity?

Rasher didn't simply enjoy inflicting physical misery on others. He liked to demonstrate his control over them first, the ability to pick at their fears and insecurities until they were willing to do whatever he wanted.

In the end, what he settles on is, he's going to get me to kill *him*. It is so diabolical, for I moment I have to admire him. Rasher may not want to die, but he's determined I'm at least going to try. On this night, it might not even be difficult. He knew I was terrified of him. All he had to do was coax me a bit.

The first thing he does is be nice. Not only does he volunteer for all the camp-pitching chores, but he acts as if I, by standing around keeping watch, am doing far more valuable and dangerous work. What he's really doing is making me see how unessential I am to his survival.

I know if I let him assemble the defense barrier by himself, he'll construct a death trap. But to be allowed to participate, I nearly have to resort to threats. We argue, I become the aggressor. A wounded look appears on his face. I know he's acting—Rasher could only ever act—but he's right, he's done nothing blameworthy. I'm angry but afraid to express that anger: the last thing I want is to be baited into giving him an excuse.

Something is bothering me. It grates on my nerves, though it's hours before I realize what it is. He's been calling me Timothy—not Timtim or TEEM! or Grimorgry or Tee-MAH—just my plain name, like a goddamn human being. I want to punch him in the throat.

We finally come to blows over the dinner. I have the K-rations in one hand, the can opener in the other. I feel his arms enveloping me from behind. Softly he's taking them away, so I knock him back.

"I was just offering to do it for you, Timothy."

"Don't act all hurt," I sneer.

"But I am hurt," he whimpers. "You bloodied my lip, Timothy. Look." He touches his mouth and shows me his fingers. The tips are red.

I don't believe I hit him in the face, I'm suspicious. I try to see the wound on his mouth.

For half a second—even less—Rasher flashes his smile.

I grab his collar and draw back a fist. Like that, the knife is out, the glint flashing in his eye, and I know not to fight him.

His body hasn't even tensed under my grip.

"Let's cool it, Timothy," he says. "You're too jittery to eat just now. It'll give you indigestion. How 'bout we go for a walk?"

"Who'll watch the camp?" I ask stupidly.

"If the bugs attack, it won't hardly matter. Come, it's a loooovey night."

Lovey? Temperatures had dropped below freezing, and the sky was obscured by putrid smoke rising from the port. But if a walk would keep him where I could see him . . .

We headed up the cliff to watch the assault on Port Benandante. I don't know why, but if you have no attachment to a place, it's a comfort to watch cities burn. Besides the occasional structural collapse or explosion, I could hear nothing but the chirping of crickets.

Rasher, sensing my thoughts drift to the captured members of our team, placed a light hand on my shoulder. "Of all the killbug horrors, there's nothing like crickets, huh? All the rest will kill you or seed you or tear you to pieces, but crickets are the only killbugs that will drag you home, throw you in a cage, and keep you alive. For entertainment. Sick, right? If they tortured you for information, well that's war. But they just want to hear you scream. For fear, for pain, for joy, they don't care. It's all music to them. Just don't ever let a cricket catch you not screaming. Scream for your ice cream, scream while you eat it, hell, better scream in your sleep. But don't go hoarse! Don't lose your voice. Because when you can no longer shout, that's . . ." Here he began to rub my back. "That's when you'll really wish you could."

"Rasher, you're Satan himself," I said.

"Nope! But I'm his besssst friend."

On the beach below, the sand seemed alive under the light of the port fire. Trapped between our reinforcements and the fortification walls, the nimmercrays were readying themselves to mount their last assault. In ecstasy, they were preparing to die.

Through a cloud of fear, I too began to accept the inevitability of death. All I had left now was to take Rasher with me. But I knew as soon as I tried, that was the end of me.

"I was underwater too long," he said suddenly. "Back when we were kids? You killed me that day. Not nearly. *Dead.* But the devil saved me."

"I wish to God the devil hadn't," I told him.

Tears started to pour down Rasher's face, "Noooo, don't say that, Teem-oh-they. Never say that. The devil saved you too, don't you see? *You too.*"

"Why would he do that?" I asked. "Why would he spare either of us?"

Rasher embraced me suddenly, burying his salty-snot face in my shirt. "'Cause we're his ickle buddies, Phthimothy. You and me. His faaaavorites."

"Cut it out."

"To be honest," he whispered, "I think he likes you . . . a *little* better!" He giggled. My body clenched as he squeezed me tighter. "Thaaaat's why he told me to give you *this.*"

I felt the force of his fist in my gut. My legs were cut from under me, and suddenly I was lying on my back with my head dangling off the cliff. He had his knees on my elbows and the blade of his knife at my scalp, ready to peel my skull like a potato. The look on his face was terror, like he was grasping someone about to fall and he couldn't hold out any longer.

He planted a wet kiss on my mouth, erupting into peals of laughter. "Mwah!"

Grabbing me by the uniform, he threw me back across the dirt, hurling his knife after my head. It just grazed my ear. With a leap, he was on top of me again. He fetched his knife and licked the blade clean—blood, dust, and all.

"Mwah mwah mwah, says the devil. Mwahahaha! Were you afraid? You were. Ohhhh, you *were*! Mwhee hee hee!"

The devil did like Gil Rasher. That was a fact. Think of all the impossible scrapes Rasher got into over the years, how he'd always survive wearing that slick smile of his. The little wink and wave he'd give us, that flash of tooth and knife that meant Remember folks, Gilbert Rasher never dies.

"Oop! Juuuust missed," he'd whisper to me on these occasions. Conspiratorially, as if he'd done something naughty. "*Has* to miss, though, Imma live forever! Aaaand I have you to thank, Misssster Archon. You baptized me, consecrated me to the hornéd one. It was all you, tee hee! And do you know who the hornéd one is? I mean, you know *of* him, but do you *know* him? Would you recognize him if you saw him? Who is he? (Who who?) Don't you know? Ohhhh, I think you do. The *bugs* know who. So should . . . you! Hee!"

That night up in the cliffs of Walpurga, he crouched beside me where I lay in the dirt, gazing out over the carnage below. He got out his whetstone and began to work his knife with it.

"It really is a beauty-ful night, isn't it, Grimgrim? Those *beastly* nimmerbugs are all gonna get *squished*, and we can watch the whole thing from here. Plus, you and I finally get to play again. When was the last time we played together? We used to be buds, yeah? It's almost like you have been"—his voice dropped a couple octaves—"avoiding me."

It's true, Rasher and I had been friends as kids, to the extent Rasher had friends. Or I had friends. We would torture cats together. I would cry and he'd laugh. It was fun. Or he'd smash traffic signals and blame me for it. After I got grounded, he'd woo me back by calling me names and we began another cycle of mischief and blame. This appealed to me. I always felt nostalgia for those days, even when I was determined to kill him.

Down on the beach, the nimmercrays' war-singers were beginning to tune up. The photino centrifuges answered with their mournful hum as our artillery came online. Rasher applauded energetically. "Look, it's staaaarting! How should we celebrate? Oh, I know, I'll tell a story. You'll like it, it's about you! Well, you're in it anyway. Mostly, it's the one about me living forever."

Well, Gentlemen, yesterday the killbugs told us a different story, the one where he doesn't.

You remember earlier in the morning, of course, Rasher at mess, giggling hysterically, his knife shoveling K-ration pellets into his mouth so a few spilled out the corner. The whole thing was hilarious.

"You're all gonna diiiie," he said. Like he was *embarrassed* for us. "So soon. Wait till you see how. Oh, the irony of it! You survive ten months on this rock, bug shit up to your eyeballs, then suddenly every last bastard of you smeared . . ." Here his knife helicoptered over his head. ". . . in one. Fell. Swoop. (Whoosh!) Everybody *dead*. Except for me. The devil's best buddy!"

The real irony is, that's gonna be the only memory of him where I'll feel sorry for the son of a bitch. Got himself smeared that very afternoon.

Ever since we landed on Thisone, the bugs seemed to pay him no mind, no matter what abuses he inflicted upon them. Then yesterday, they smote him like as if noticing him for the first time. The moment one stuck its pointy bits in, the rest swarmed and sliced him open, patiently taking fire while a junehorn caught his blood in its mandible, boiling and congealing it. As this pudding got passed around, the bugs prostrated themselves in the dirt and gore, offering up a strange plaintive cry.

All my years in the infantry, I've never heard a killbug plaintive about anything. Or seen hesitation in its movement. It's their decisiveness that trumps the technological edge we hold over them. But as they killed and ate Rasher, I felt a schism within them.

Something on Rasher's face changed too. I'd assumed living forever was just a threat to agitate people, but yesterday he puzzled at the gash in his chest like he was suddenly in the wrong body. He turned toward me and mouthed his last words, which I didn't catch with all the blood bubbling out. But, I understood: at that moment, his confusion far outstripped his agony.

Rasher really believed the bugs had consecrated him.

"You oughta know all about it," he said that night above Port Benandante, "you were there. But you don't remember. You spotted a ripe conch fruit in a tree, and you scurried up to shake it loose. Instead, you brought a hornets' nest down on your head. Jackass. Only no angry swarm inside. A beige gas came out instead, and you crumpled to the ground. A couple twitches and you lay still. Dead as a knob, I thought. No pulse!

"While I was going through your stuff, a killbug tottered out of the jungle on its hind legs, prancing high, knees up like a drum major. Kinda wobbly. It had wormy lips twice as wide as its fat head and wore its antennae up and to the side, kinda like it had a feather in its cap. It examined you where you lay, then came right up to me. The meat fissure it had for a mouth stretched even wider, like it's trying to smile, revealing huge square teeth and—get this—a tongue! It stared a bit, tilted its head to one side, like it's trying to be cute, you know? Then it put a foreleg forward, held out its wings, and dipped for a little curtsy. Suddenly something deep inside it started to boil. 'Hail!' I heard it say."

"You understand bug?" I asked.

"No, it spoke human," Gil said. "It had the . . . apparatus. It told me that's what the freak mouth was for, to form human words when the Hive wants to speak to us.

"'Then why have I never heard killbugs talk before?' I asked.

"It stretched its rictus wide again. 'Till now the war has spoken for us,' it said.

"'What, like in corpses?' I asked.

"'Yes!' it screeched, looking very pleased.

"'Well,' I said, 'what now? Did you develop a stutter?'

"It made a bubbly sound, like giggles but from its anterior. Lots of little farts. 'Since the birth of the galaxy,' it said, 'war has been our communion with the Two-Legs. The Hive's sacred duty is to destroy the Two-legs, utterly, bit-t-t-terly.' It bent over at the thorax, all the way down and stayed there. 'It is the Two-legs who has gone silent.

Your servant invites the Two-legs to begin the dialog of war again. What the Two-legs commands, the Hive obeys!'

"The killbug's huge lips kept working near the dirt, even when it wasn't talking. 'What are you doing,' I asked, 'eating shit?'

"'Bowing,' it said, 'before the . . . the *Death-namer!*' Its whole body thrashed head to tail.

"'What's a Death-namer?' I asked.

"Its stubby man-legs thumped the ground. 'The Death-namer is the Two-Legs in whose name the Queen reigns, by whose command the Queen makes suns tremmmmbl-l-l-e.' It quaked and shrieked both times it said Queen. 'As the Death-namer commands the Hive, the Hive shall be the Wrecker of Worlds. The Death-namer' (I swear it was orgasming every time it said the word) 'shall choose in what order the stars go dark.'

"'And why,' I asked, just to watch its crazy tongue-thing work, 'why does the Death-namer give these orders?'

"'The Death-namer *wants* it!'

"This time, the exoskeleton rattled so violently, it fell over, so I helped it back up. 'Thank you,' it said, making an ancient Earth gesture I believe means Go stick it in your ass.

"'Fuck you too,' I offered.

"'Oh, most gracious! Your servant bows to you, bows before the Death-namer!' The screech was so deafening, Tim, I don't know how it didn't wake you, dead or otherwise. 'The Death-namer gives council to the Hive,' the killbug continued, 'and glory to the Queen! The Death-namer burrrrns with *wrath* at the galaxy.'

"'Sure,' I said.

"'One by one,' it continued, 'he names them. One by one, the Hive rends and consumes them, scorches them with fire, smothers them in black smoke.'

"'Oh, I like this guy!' I said.

"Its funny little legs pounded a war march in place. 'Today the Death-namer has been chosen. The Hive worships and obeys the Death-namer, and he is immortal! The Death-namer lives until the galaxy goes dark!'"

Here Gil blushed and giggled before continuing.

"'Are you called something, killbug?' I asked.

"It said Harry or some dumb thing.

"'Harry,' I asked, 'Did you just spend a lifetime practicing at being Harry for just this moment?'

"'Yes,' Harry said, 'I studied at Two-legs very hard!'

"I wondered just how much it knew. 'Show me, Harry,' I said. 'Can you do this? Can you dance the mashed potato?' I started bopping around. But the poor bastard's huge stupid head threw off its center of gravity, so I grabbed it by the arms and spun it around a few times. 'Shtaaaat shpreadin' da nooz!' I sang. It was fucking thrilled. The foxtrot it could do, the foxtrot it *knew*. We cut a nice little rug around and around your body. If you hadn't been dead at the moment, I'd have roused you to join us.

"'Death to the galaxy!' I shouted.

"Harry was so happy it sprayed shit all over the place. 'Yes, yes!' it burbled.

"'The Death-namer lives forever,' I called.

"Harry farted with glee. 'May the Hive Queen bite off your asshole!' it replied.

"'Hey, Harry,' I said.

"'Yes?' said Harry.

"'Your name is Harry,' I said.

"'Yes,' it said.

"Then I cut its fucking head off. No protest either: it called it a privilege to die in the Death-namer's presence. Meant it too, as far as I could tell. So I did a nice thing. It might not have been a good idea to murder an envoy direct from the Queen, but like, what the fuck is going to happen? The Death-namer lives forever!"

Rasher elbowed me in the ribs.

He and I looked out together over the cliff. The

nimmercrays had finished their pre-battle festivities and were launching their assault on the port. The sea too had roused itself to batter the harbor walls, as if the whole galaxy was swelling with euphoria over the coming ruin. On the horizon, the sun bled like a ruptured boil, and I could almost see Gil and his freak killbug dancing a skater's step across the gruesome sky.

Years ago, when Earth had gotten ashed, Rasher told me it wasn't the end of the world. "Don't fuss. All this means now is a war. We're long overdue. They're healthy you know. Lots of bad mojo builds up during peace. Too much prosperity and civilization becomes unbearable: all those social abstractions and high ideals, people start sensing they're bullshit. Year after year of saying please and thank you while getting scratched a thousand times over and pretending it never bleeds—people yearn to indulge in what's physical and real. All the buried appetites no one likes to give name to—the urge to murder, rob, burn, rape, torture and terrorize—these are inhuman things the human animal does to feel alive. War is their holiday. And the outcome is constructive. Wait and see. We'll be better for this in the end."

I'm still certain it was Rasher who poisoned the water at Ethos Post. We blamed the killbugs because we found their pods near the treatment hatch. But why would killbugs leave pods there? People have this idea they shit larvae everywhere they go. They don't. But we had no evidence against Rasher. Plus, didn't he drink it too and get as sick as the rest of us? Somehow his illness refuted our suspicion. But that was the thrill for him! Because Rasher knew firsthand how severe our agony was. Physical pain didn't mean to him what it means to most of us. Nothing you did to his body could compare to the ravages inside— if anything, it distracted from the hell within. That's my theory anyway.

I often wonder about the meaning of lives like Rasher's. Why does our society allow for creatures so fundamentally monstrous? When we stand near them, we don't feel the presence of another human soul, yet we are powerless to do anything about them. We don't kill them or cast them out or take away their parking privileges. Think of all the petty reasons people are stigmatized, ostracized, or persecuted, while people like Rasher are always allowed to live among us, even rule over us. The thought of doing without them makes us nervous, as if we might need them to get through some brutal upcoming winter. I never killed Rasher—neither did any of you—but not for fear of punishment, not out of conscience. I always chose, dangerous as he was, to let him live. What did he represent that I couldn't bring myself to destroy?

Whatever the qualm was, Rasher was aware of it. He counted on it and tested its limits constantly. High in the cliffs above Port Benandante, he injected me with fear, drop by drop, teasing me closer to the edge of my sanity.

Look out that way, out over there.

His spidery fingers crawled up my back till I felt a gentle tap-tap-tap. *Your heart is here,* he seemed to say. It was transparent to him, not just the organ, but all my needs, insecurities, and yearnings. The way he could unveil my most buried desires made my skin grew hot with shame and indignation. Why should this superior perception come so effortlessly to Rasher, capable only of using it to treat people as playthings?

I ought to destroy this abomination while I have the chance, I thought. Up here beyond the reach of human society and its laws, I needed to make sure that one day he didn't end up on Thisone Rock, terrorizing and tormenting us for his perverse amusement. The impulse to be free of Rasher and the fear he inspired threaded itself tighter inside me. From the soft smile on his face, I knew he sensed he was winning his little game. I needed to strike before he knew he'd already won.

"Remember," he whispered, the heat of his breath upon my neck, "thaaaat's how it works: you snoozed, now I live forever!"

I pounced—it was reflex. Rasher sidestepped me cleanly, and with a glint, the knife was out. If its blade touched me even once, I knew a slow death awaited me. I attempted to disarm him with the maneuver we learned in boot camp, the one Rasher could elude in his sleep. To my surprise, I felt his wrist twist under mine and saw the knife fall to the ground.

"Oops!" He giggled, his expression almost cocky. My sense of victory turned to terror.

The hesitation cost me a blow to the solar plexus, and Rasher escaped toward the brush. I followed on his heels. With a leap, I snared his ankle and pulled him to the ground. We wrestled. He bit me and almost escaped, but a clean blow to the head knocked the fight out of him.

I pondered what to do with his limp body. I might tie him up and wait for evac. But why? Because I'm afraid of him, this slippery little man? The idea made me so furious, I dragged him towards the cliff's edge, resolved to throw him to the nimmercrays—one last treat before the cannon devoured them all. There would be no inquiry.

Down below, the bugs crashed like ripples against the

fortifications. Despite their frenzy, the collective movement was ordered and beautiful, as if the galaxy had created them exactly for this. The fusion glow from our artillery batteries flashed atop the ramparts, and as the explosions pounded their ranks, cratering the shore, and raining bits of exoskeleton upon the sand, this too seemed patterned and graceful, an insane orgy directed by an invisible hand. Twisted and awful and meant-to-be.

One more body, I thought. Just another speck of dust tossed into a cyclone.

Rasher glanced down at the carnage below, then up at me. "Please," he said. Just a single word: no tears, no argument, no resistance. Please. My knuckles tightened on his collar, and in the back of my throat I tasted bile. This soulless creature, who has never feared death, for whom no emotion has ever lain behind his vacant eyes, said "please" and suddenly it was impossible to kill him. God only knows why.

I helped him to his feet and pushed him roughly toward the campsite. When he dragged his feet, I thumped him with an open hand against the back of the head. It knocked him stupid, but he reveled in it: it signified his complete victory over me. I had tried to murder him, but I simply did not have his permission. He lay on the ground too stunned to stand, drunk on the hilarity of it all.

Rasher was elated, not because he survived but because he won. Until the evac came, he said please for everything. He asked for things just so he could say please. "Can you reboot the gluon ionizers, *please?*" He had found his magic word. With every iteration, he grew bigger, I got smaller.

After we rejoined the others, he and I were assigned to the mop-up force. I nearly went down under friendly fire three or four times. I'm not sure Rasher meant to miss.

And now I've outlived him. Is such a thing possible?

As a war bard, Peter Anglewood once sought a poetic model that forewent the usual hominid nonsense about our civilization's superiority, and focused instead on celebrating the war itself. Hand to hand or at a distance, mortal conflict ignited a fire that illuminated the beauty of the galaxy. That's why Pete chose Gil as his template for the ideal soldier. In reality, Gil was not so sanitary or symmetrical, but Anglewood didn't care. Gilbert Rasher served as the gritty framework Peter could hang his vision upon.

Remember how Anglewood described his final artistic phase as "tuning killbug joy to human lyre?" He wrote that poem called "The Scalpel: St. Gilbert's Day," where he beatified Rasher and made the knife Rasher's sacred attribute. In the poem, Anglewood declared life the "disease of matter," and Rasher its doctor. "Listen," he has Rasher say, "to the coughs and sputters of our galaxy. Repugnant infection and malignant growths riddle her star systems. But I, at last, bring true healing. Aiding her immunity, I destroy foreign bodies hostile to her welfare. When I finish my cure, nothing will be left to put her at risk."

Pete made death Rasher's message and mission.

> Flash, his steel a guiding star
> Flash, let hand and feeler follow
> Flash, a scalpel's dance across the synapse of space
> Restoring cosmic bodies to primordial perfection

> Imprint its shape upon every heart
> With this I kill, by this I die
> Until the Queen rots in the peace of death
> Let the trumpets sound—to war, to war!
> May every leg twitch, then fall still

But what did Gil believe? Belief is a subclass of emotion, I think, and he had only a facsimile of those.

Which made Rasher the only free one among us. Some call the body the spirit's prison, but often Gil made me wonder if the real confinement is our humanity—our sense of obligation and our need for acceptance. And—oh my God!—all that useless fear. For safety, for family, for reputation, for sanity: most people can't imagine a day without fear. But what does it ever accomplish beyond making us wretched? When I saw that Rasher could lay all that fear down, I confess I felt a twinge of envy. Is that so strange?

On the other hand, I believe people like Rasher are why human beings have clung to the idea of a devil. Disease, earthquakes, blighted crops—even primitives could endure these things without imagining some supernatural sadist who dispenses misfortune. But to explain Rasher, humanity had to invent *evil*. I believe the devil began as an ordinary sociopath. In stories, people try to outsmart him, but the devil always gets the better of them in the end. Why? Because he doesn't want anything, not even not to lose. If he was motivated by hatred, you could find a way to use him to your advantage, but he's *bored*, and the only thing that satisfies him is something he's never seen before. The galaxy is replete in nothing so much as the variety of human misery.

My comrades-in-arms, Revenant of Beta, killbugs watch us from the hills and smell us from under the earth. Their sentries circle the skies above, yet once again this morning a tranquil sun has risen upon us. Every day, twice a day, the mantes bear our assaults almost patiently, like Cerberus tolerating the incessant yapping of a terrier.

For all Gilbert Rasher's threats and promises of death, it is only now that I stand before his lifeless body do I feel we have reached the precipice of their fulfillment. I've been unable to shake the suspicion that the overwhelming bug presence has spared us for the sake of just one man. That man cannot be other than he in whose name they found it a pleasure to kill and by whose hand they believed it a privilege to die.

Despite this, I feel no dread. The endless expectation of doom has so frayed my nerves, I can only feel impatience for the hammer to fall. In my bones, I know we have outlived our chance for salvation. The evil of this place no longer merely surrounds us but dwells inside us. If in a few weeks the ships return on schedule and carry us away, then we will bear that evil back with us to the fleet. Better to die with it here, better to die!

Rasher, god damn it, Gil, why didn't you destroy us all first?

Ad saeculum saeculorum. Whatever the hell that means. Amen.

THE DEATH OF HARVEY CROOP

YESTERDAY WE LOST A RUDDER. Although I have faith in Captain Prescott to steer us safely until the ships return, it will be difficult for anyone to wield the moral authority of Major Croop. Harvey Croop assembled this amalgam of castoff Betan scraps into a deadly and durable apparatus. He taught us how to persevere on the jungle asteroids, the swamp worlds, the ice rocks, the desert systems. Despite efforts, both within and without our ranks, to erode morale and eradicate our sense of purpose, Croop got his men through it, day by day, hour by hour.

When we landed on Thisone, tactics for assaulting a mantis nest had not yet been developed. It's clear the brass made no attempt to learn how to dismantle the factories on this rock, or else they would have armed us differently.

With just a handful of heliophaze chlorocutters instead of all these up-down quark reversers, we might've had a chance at carrying out our mission. But it was Croop who noticed the mantes are genetically averse to guarding the sloops. To them, nothing in its right mind would crawl up those tunnels but docile shit harvesters. Their tactical algorithms fail at every pass to discern a plausible advantage for a human infantryman to crawl under sixty pounds of gear up an avalanche of rolling filth, so we've managed to minimize our casualties.

The mantis algorithm overlooks this because it can't fathom any attack strategy where the primary objective is no casualties, because the best way to achieve this would be *no assault*. But Harvey Croop knew that eleven months on this fecal hellscape with nothing to direct your efforts, you maggots would inevitably slaughter each other. Since crawling up shit sloops every day was the one tactic too irrational for the killbugs to counter, it heretofore has been our salvation.

We have toiled for so long under the Major's leadership, it's easy to forget how back on Beta, Harvey Croop was the greengrocer. He sold us tomacinis, toadplantains, kaprabellos, chimbokchokes, candyroots, and camelblatt. Before the Earth was ashed, the most warlike action he ever performed was to spritz the halepoppers to keep them moist. Who imagined that one day he would marshal us into shit sloops every morning at dawn, every evening at dusk, and we would rely on his booming voice to lead us back out again?

Then last night, death laid low our noble commander! Croop was standing atop a belt-high mound of bug filth, while behind him, our ordnance lit the sky. Silhouetted against the plasma pops, he shouted orders in a voice deep and brassy from disciplining generations of Beta boys outside his shop. Fuck it was loud: I couldn't understand a word he was saying. Croop gestured to me for his binoculars. As I passed them over, something heavy fell into my hands in return. I wondered why he'd given me his helmet. Then I realized his face was still attached.

A Michaelmas mosquito had flown up behind and parted his head from his shoulders with a single smooth motion. Like a gentle embrace, a loving kiss.

I stared down at the strong chin and much-broken nose, which once could tell with a whiff which gordonya beans were freshest for salads, which might be better for soup. In the plasma light, his brow furrowed as orders continued issuing from beneath his wiry mustache. "Filthy cunt-faced, manure-slurping, thrapple-fuckers." Those were his last words.

. . . Or "Never give up, fight to the last," one of the two.

As a child, Harvey Croop was frequently ill. The fourth or fifth doctor he visited belonged to the Bluebuster political fringe which argued that the extraction of ragnarite was destroying Beta, the trade of ragnarite was destroying the Alliance, and the use of ragnarite was destroying the galaxy. She claimed Croop suffered malnourishment from the consumption of food created synthetically as the byproduct of ragnarite refinement. She prescribed a diet of the canned lentils brought over to Beta by the earliest pioneers.

Encouraged by the result of the doctor's treatment, Croop started his own breadbasket movement at eighteen. In small underground greenhouses, he experimented with the cultivation of grains and herbs.

"Food grown in the dirt?" people said. "What are we, primitives? Is that even sanitary? This is how plagues are spread!"

Croop said our synthetic foodstuffs were deficient in proteins and others vital compounds, so we'd be healthier if we grew our own. Not only that, they would taste better. "Eating doesn't have to be unpleasant!" he said.

"Blasphemy," people cried. "If God wanted us to enjoy food, he wouldn't have put our mouths so close to our noses where we have to smell it too."

In addition to nutritional benefit, research suggested that the agricultural process could even help tame the meteorological conditions that made life on Beta's surface so brutal. At twenty-four, after years of odd jobs to pay for seed, equipment, and interworld queries on botany and agriculture, Harvey Croop left the ragnarite mines and went to work Beta's topsoil, in which he planted cedarbeets, ochrifal, and other hardy vegetables. Conditions under the Betan sky were harsh, but he swore to produce some proper food or die trying.

After atmospheric conditions poisoned his fourth season of crops, he moved back into the shafts and began a vegetable import business, bringing in tubers, roots, and leafy greens from around the galaxy.

For a long time, no one ate the vegetables besides Croop, but then people noticed he wasn't developing that unfortunate condition with its drastic sexual side effect from which nearly all Betan men over thirty suffer—let's not speak its name. Croop insisted all it took was adding torpalbaters to your diet. Well, never mind the smell, males from ten to senility started binging on them in the street.

And baters were a gateway veg: soon we saw no end to the disgusting leafy things that snuck their way onto our plates under the pretext they offered some hormonal supercharge.

Business boomed. Just a half ton of refined ragnarite purchased domestically could be traded on the galactic market for a whole cargo hold of gaddersnips. Ideologically, Croop was against the ragnarite trade, but when we confronted the avowed Bluebuster on his apparent hypocrisy (because we're bastards, not because we took issue), he agreed proliferating ragnarite bent his principles, but since the mineral was destined to end up everywhere eventually, the proceeds might as well benefit health back home. "For better or for worse," he said, "I am, and always will be, a Son of Beta."

Let his detractors say what they will, no one could overlook the personal sacrifice Croop made for his dietary vision. In exchange for the minuscule slice of the Consortium's export monopoly which had allowed him to finance his business, Harvey Croop submitted to conjugal duty with Kegger Pelt's physically and socially repugnant eldest daughter. Not even bwain damage, if you know what I'm saying.

But soon the newly-founded Dietary Authority bought

out Croop's suppliers and his business nearly tanked. Croop managed to stay afloat by supplying several leafies that had no purported super-benefits. They simply tasted good, which suited homemakers who hadn't had their palettes mangled by a lifetime of rag farming.

Then Earth was destroyed. Even while we were still getting the orbital images of the whole rock covered in impenetrable black smoke, Croop advised against Beta going to war. Any human was superior to the finest insect, he said, but humanity simply could not compete with the killbugs in military lasting power to make war a tenable solution. Crackers, I know, but after the vote went through, he still enlisted to save his nephew, Shem, from his shaft-domestic's recruitment quota.

To the surprise of many, including himself, he scored well on the infantry's aptitude tests and was recommended for officer training. He declined at first, saying the idea of one man holding rank over another repulsed him. He eventually complied because too few Betan men of his life experience hadn't been near crippled from labor in the mines. "We need you," they said, "however grudgingly, you leaf-eating lunatic."

The first year of the war seemed to swat'n'smear all the Beta boys except us delinquents. Our rock alone lost fifty thousand at Withered Skrall, eighty thousand at Porkhat Peak, seventy more at Umpteenth Atoll. I can't even breathe aloud how many of the Pride of Beta a single hour of devastation laid low at Gretzen Ahdagh. The bravest and most noble among us fared the worst. You had to have something a little wrong with you to survive. Or else you did now. Few men would have had the acumen to organize the remainder of us into a highway cleaning crew, let alone a disciplined fighting force.

"No footman faultier than the Beta boys," recruiters complained. "They live like cavemen on their blasted rock, the richest and most powerful as filthy and stupid as the rest of them. So primitive, they probably still worship fire. Those feral brats can't even understand ideas like loyalty, camaraderie, discipline, or honor. They shovel better than average, though, so let them terraform some shitpits or something. They don't swim so bad either. Maybe they can drown themselves building bridges over the Straits of Velcron. Just don't let those sadistic man-children near any weapons. And whatever you do, split them up! Their shoddiness increases exponentially in groups."

What had we done that the brass thought we were no longer good enough even to get blown up?

The most strenuous battle Harvey Croop ever fought

was to uphold our enlistment and keep us out of the Alliance's infamous labor battalions. After completing his regular duties, then-Captain Croop spent every spare minute sucking up to majors, petitioning colonels, begging audiences with generals. He languished in waiting rooms, wording and rewording petitions, finding ways to put a better spin on our dubious performance record. Eventually, Croop's request was taken into consideration and a decision was made. He lined us all up so he could unseal the message in front of us. One unit, one fate. His eyes were expressionless as they surveyed the text.

"Congratulations," he said, "you are going back to war."

His booming voice barely audible, his eyes scarcely leaving the floor, he told us it had been his duty to see that his men were treated like soldiers. Beta born, he owed it to the Beta boys who had grown up around his shop to ensure we had the opportunity to stand up like men for whatever moment fate allowed. By virtue of our innate human dignity, that right belonged to us.

Then Croop cleared his throat.

"That, at least, was what I kept telling myself. You little bastards tried to burn down my shop at least once a year. You think I don't know who? I could give names. And dates! Your parents tried to convince me it was the trade syndicate upset I wouldn't honor the unofficial embargo on Perpetua Prime, but I know it was you snot-noses who didn't like the smell of boiled starkradish at their dinner tables. I could have taken a year's vacation with the money I spent protecting my shop from you little terrorists. I wanted to scorch your eyes out with a red-hot mulch fork, but what would have been the point? You're all from endless lines of little brothers, each nastier and more spiteful than the last. Any justice I took out on you, you would have repaid on me tenfold.

"And what you did to me was nothing compared to the way you treat each other. Who else do you lumpy ass-bleeders have besides yourselves? Do you think anyone is itching to make friends with the Beta boys, so undisciplined they can't play a sport with real rules? Frolicking. You slosh around in four feet of water, jumping and yelling arbitrarily to announce you've scored. In the real galaxy, you have to put a ball in a net and someone tries to stop you. There's work involved! But no one could be bothered to referee you brats. You're less interested in the score than in tormenting whichever poor sap you chose to bully within an inch of suicide.

"You can't imagine how many times I reconsidered my choice to petition our leadership to put weapons back in your hands—which, by the way, is conditional on me accepting a promotion to sign on as your commander and trust you not to set fire to me in my sleep! What I did for you, I did for my own conscience, to convince myself I believed the spark of humanity could still be fanned into flame somewhere in this—let's face it—inherently vicious galaxy. Or at least, that I had the strength to behave as if I believed.

"I have to tell you, as hard as I worked for you, some part of me wanted to see the word 'denied' stamped in red letters across my petition. Well, congratulations, request granted. The human race is willing to readmit you on a probationary basis.

"What this means, in practical terms, is this will be the death of you. A quick end to this conflict can only mean the utter annihilation of humanity, so all you can hope for—the best you can do—is to hold the torch until the yet unimagined weapon capable of winning this war has been developed. Your death will be painful, messy, covered in filth, and serving no obvious purpose. But you were born unworthy of bearing a name and have done little since to improve your condition. You have maybe a few months—with an impossible stroke of luck, a few years—

to rectify this. I have scant optimism this shall occur. May I not live long enough to see myself proven correct."

The silence that followed was excruciating. With his jaw clenched, Croop made his way around the room, casting his hard gaze at every eye. Behind his terrible countenance, boiling with its tacit threats, was a plea: 'Please, gentlemen, Storm of Beta, validate the sacrifice I have made today. Let me go to my grave comforted that the burden I choose to bear in life will have redeemed me in the end.' It was the only time I've seen Harvey Croop truly vulnerable.

Then, without a word of dismissal, he turned on his heel and walked out. That was a lifetime and God knows how many worlds ago.

So, what does the loss of Harvey Croop mean for our mission?

It's little more than two weeks till the ships return, if they return. Should our frontier be collapsing no faster than at the rate when we were deployed, the fleet may still send someone to rescue us. If not, we will never see human civilization again.

The Major marshaled us up the sloops every day to dismantle the combat factory of the Great Dane-sized mantes on Thisone rock, the third or fourth largest mantis factory in the galaxy. Despite our efforts, we believe their numbers are actually increasing. We didn't crawl through shit for the glory of the infantry, for the honor of Beta, or even for the salvation of humankind. We did it because, under the leadership of Major Croop, those daily missions made us men, kinda. Every day, twice a day (I still can't believe we went three times on Christmas), while we were trying to kill those nasty horned bastards, we acted as a unit, with purpose. Instead of simply waiting here to die.

Well, what do we do now? Do we press on with our mission? Before you answer, let's remember, we have no idea why the bugs haven't launched a full offensive and overwhelmed us. Outside our twice daily runs, we have fought only skirmishes, most of which we instigated by accident. This morning I heard grumbling among you. You swear you have crawled up the sloops for the last time. You say you braved the mantes for Croop, but you won't for anyone else. A few have said we ought to keep fighting so as not to appear vulnerable, but that's enough sloops and mantis scythes. Let's smear harpsipedes: they make that hilarious singsong sound when you tag one through the eye. If we have to die, let's do it not covered in bugshit. Let's go out with our junk on, like men. With our faces, like people.

Others of you, an increasingly more vocal faction, have suggested we stop fighting altogether.

I disagree. I recommend continuing the mantis mission. For over ten months we have obeyed our orders to the letter. Mostly. When the ships return, we'll all receive commendations, for grit, for valor, for maintaining military bearing under deplorable conditions cut off from our chain of command. Shall we throw all that aside, hard-bought with a year of sweat and blood, just to evade a couple dozen more sloop runs?

Well, don't everybody think about it.

Comrades, consider the sacrifices Harvey Croop made to mold us into the soldiers we've become. If not for him, we'd be breaking our backs shoveling shit on Cordon Blanc. Okay, yes, we shoveled shit today, and most shit shovelers on Cordon Blanc die with their balls on, but how many die the toughest sumbitches in the infantry? How many of them, day in and day out, stick the muzzle of their muon defrazgulators up the rectum of the most gruesome cuntmunchers in the galaxy? You may feel you'd sooner die than do this another day, but think! When those ships return us to the fleet, who the hell is gonna fuck with us? Won't it be worth a few more days of this hell to watch our fellows step back in awe as we walk past all a-cocked and - peepered? The baddest motherfuckers in uniform!

Come on, lemme hear you say boo. Let's hear what it'll sound like when your mere breath makes men tremble. Let's hear the hell-flung sound that will blow back those milk-toothed recruits in knock-kneed fear. All those pissants from the sunshine worlds who have looked down on us for so long—let's hear the sound that will straighten their backs and lower their eyes in wonder at our heavy, low-hanging, free-swinging rag rocks. Let's hear it!

On three, 'kay? One, two—

All right, let's try something else.

Think of when the war is over and we go home to Beta

. . .

Okay, never mind that.

My comrades-in-arms, what are your lives worth to you? What would you give to see another sunrise? All your worldly goods? A limb? No. Shoot me now, is what you'd say. But what have you seen up those dark tunnels that you still fear? What can happen in there you haven't dreamt about and flailed over so many nights it'd almost come as a relief?

Brothers, there's little chance of victory, scant hope for human survival. We have nothing left except the dignity

Harvey Croop planted in us. Through duty and toil and blood, it has taken root. If we are destined to die on this rock, let's die with that. Let's make the one good thing we ever did honoring the memory of the man who honored us. Amidst all this shit, that one clump of gold remains within our reach. So, let's not pass it up. Let's hold on to it dearly.

You'd rather die holding your dicks. I appreciate that, you're attached to them. And who am I to ask anything of you? Nearly everyone who has died here has died spitting distance from me, half the time by a scythe or spore missile that would have been the death of me if not for his body shielding mine.

Actually, that's peculiar, now that I think about it. I wonder why—

Okay! Mutiny it is! I'm with you guys.

But gentlemen, before you leave today, I'd like to address you formally in case no other opportunity arises. Oi! What have you got to do today, you're all just retired! Please, I'll be brief. Sit.

The galaxy, I've discovered, is a playing field of futility. The Hominid Alliance has marshaled us to save the universe, while the enemy is sworn to destroy it. But deep in my bones, I know nothing will be accomplished except all of us making a great muck of it. The soldiers and ships fighting today will not survive this war, but life in the galaxy will, and nothing either side can do will change that. We die, life continues. Sounds almost idiotic.

The individual might ask, then, why toil? Why struggle if the outcome is already inevitable? Because amid this uproar and upheaval, we can choose to become, if even for a moment, human beings truly worthy of the name—though we can be sure, however long that moment lasts, it will be forgotten. But in that moment, you and I shall see—who knows, even the departing spirit of Harvey Croop may see—that for an eternity lasting no longer than the break of one wave upon the shore and the next, that we were men full of courage, dignity, and—yes, I'll say it, close as we are to the end (No, not vim!)—full of love.

Comrades, there are so few of us left, no more than a quarter, and not the best. We have lost the strongest, bravest, smartest. The most cunning, the most eloquent, the most soulful, the most compassionate. The best leader. We are outnumbered, our tools are broken, our ammunition is depleted, and if the tide of war on distant stars has turned against us, rescue may never come.

You have spoken, we will not fight again. Instead, we huddle and await whatever destiny comes. To be honest, I dread the purplish glow of the aft thrusters appearing in orbit. Comrades-in-arms, we have had a disagreeable childhood together, full of rivalry, jealousy, spite, sabotage, and cruelty. You against me, I against you. But despite what animosity may lie buried in my bones, I could not wish the continuation of this war upon the least of you. Granule by granule, this war has worn away all the wickedness of our youth. We have earned, if not though moral courage, if not through strength of will, then simply through the daily erosion wrought by toil and suffering, the right to be reborn.

As I stand before you today, we are ashes, we are dust. Should we look now toward the skies, the only light we can hope to spy in the darkness is the spark of our own regeneration. And I do not know if such a spark even exists. Or if I want it to. Perhaps the ancients are right, the cycles of life and decay are simply a trap for our souls to escape. Perhaps this war only exists as an opportunity for escape.

Comrades, imagine if tomorrow you woke and discovered you never were. Wouldn't that be peace? Imagine at next sunrise, you have never once seen a killbug or heard of Thisone Rock. As strange as it may sound, I believe such a dawn exists. Nothing this cruel, this awful can ever be real. The answer to the oldest and greatest mystery—how can anything exist at all?—must simply be that it does not: our entire universe is merely a momentary jitter between two non-realities, particle and anti-particle perpetuating only long enough to destroy each other.

But I can't leave you with such mysticism. Instead, I'll close with a story from my youth, which ought to resonate, since it happened to all of you too.

When I was a boy, my mother sent me to Harvey Croop's grocery to pick up some asparagus for dinner. While Croop was in the back uncovering the freshest bundle for me, I was at the counter devouring as many junemint candies as I could shovel into my little maw before he returned. He came back to find me dripping with evidence of theft. Reaching for a washcloth, Croop began to clean my mouth and hands. I trembled under his ministrations, wondering if he knew what I'd done.

"Do you know what they used to call asparagus back on Earth?" he asked, giving me one of his stern looks.

I shook my head, terrified to admit I didn't know.

"Fetlish teeth were called corn," he said, "sprig's kidney was eggplant, space apples were just called apples, but asparagus . . ." Here he paused to make a broad wipe under my jaw. ". . . was called asparagus. But do you know what the ancient Greeks and Romans used to call it five thousand years ago?"

I shook my head again.

"Asparagus," he whispered, smiling faintly.

By now he had removed all the chocolate from my face. "The point of the story," he said, "in case it escapes your greedy little head, is that no matter how topsy-turvy the galaxy becomes, some things actually never change."

Picking up one of the junemint wrappers from the floor, he wrote a number on it and handed to me. "Give this to your mother. Tell her next time the usual surcharge applies. The same one she paid on account of your brother, William."

Ad saeculum saeculorum. I finally found the translation. Actually, I've been saying it wrong the entire time, it's in saecula saeculorum, "into the generations of generations." But I still don't understand what it means. Amen.

THE DEATH OF EVERYBODY

I LEAVE HERE A SUPPLEMENTARY *account of the strange case of Pvt. Timothy Archon. I have no desire to blow the whistle on every breach of military protocol or animal husbandry code which occurs on board, but as the captain and his officers will be disinclined to include certain critical matters in their official report, it may transpire that a more-assed-than-half record of events will be required for the security of the Hominid Alliance in the future.*

Only in emergency scenarios do I foresee someone dredging through the personal logs of an orderly in the medical wing of this rescue/salvage vessel. Should such contingency arise, I imagine the guilty will have already fallen beyond the reach of discipline. Should any such action be administered as result of this record, let me state such was not my intention—not that I would feel bad about it either.

I am in ideal position to document this medical anomaly. While I slosh the mop, everyone speaks as if I don't exist, and as long as I can rake up a hot tip on the legging matches, Cmdr. Griff will tell me whatever I want to know. Privy to everything, me.

This is a tale of death and ferrets. First the short version:

Our vessel, the Starboat Dennis Hickey, has traveled six weeks into killbug space to This One Rock to recover the surviving members and equipment of a mantis factory dismantlement operation. We now return to fleet with only one wounded infantryman and a hangar bay overflowing with dooking scrotum-biters. Hell to pay, us, if anyone finds out why.

Now with the juicy bits:

While aboard the last fueling station before killbug territory, Cmdr. Griff found himself in the backroom of a creamery where they wager on slommoth cage fights. Not the crowd you'd think death matches would draw. One slommoth trainer complained ever since the lady across the plaza started offering pottery lessons, no one was clamoring for slammoth anymore. However: just over the border in reclaimed space, was rumor of a kook who lived alone on a dwarf rock raising ferrets.

Ferrets very popular now, the trainer explained. On brink of extinction, humans suddenly kitsch-romantic for ferret-kind. Little ferret doctors, little ferret mimes, little ferrets in tall hats ruling over ancient Earth empires: Rome, China, Xerox. Banned for centuries as pests on most colonies. After mars-bees swarmed and obliterated the annual Weasel Admirers Galactic Gala (WAGG), the kook must own some of the last in existence. Good money for anyone who puts hands on 'em.

Not eager to enter orbit over a killbug factory, the Hickey *took a two-day detour to this dwarf rock. "Raising ferrets" did not describe: a ferret army for ferret Armageddon. Operation upscaled after Earth got ashed. Captain offered to buy or trade for a few, but the kook refused to part with a single one. Needed nothing in God's dark cosmos except his preciouses, he said. No dice, cap'n.*

A stroke of questionable inspiration: Cmdr. Griff recalled an obsolete Alliance housing regulation that prohibited more than four marsupials per non-terrestrial domicile. (Ensues: heated debate on what constitutes "terrestrial" and "marsupial.") Regulation required captain to confiscate all ferrets in excess of four. Over twenty thousand terraria in total. Holy snipe.

The kook, however, had networked his hundreds of ferret-

upkeep droids to a master self-destruct switch for just this contingency (i.e.: someone trying to steal all his ferrets). Sizzle-pop, creak, crash. Sadistic kooky grin. Meaning: we gotta care for 'em all by hand.

Correct action to liquidate the surplus. No one had the heart. Too valuable.

Problem: storage. Dormitories, hangar bay, and half the medical wing refit for ferret care. Salvage site on This One not yet reached. Who knew how many men and how much equipment to bring back? After eleven months in shadow of a killbug factory, realistic estimate: bupkis. If not, manage issue when we get there.

Meanwhile, crew advised of ferret's estimated market value and told whoever helps keep animals alive and healthy earns share of the revenue. All nonessential personnel reassigned to feeding, watering, and shit-scooping. (Inadvisable adjustment to definition of "essential.") Double shifts required.

Three weeks later. Problem: surface scans from orbit over This One reveal one hundred twelve men alive in camp, plus equipment more or less intact. Our orders to haul all back if feasible. Proper course: jettison the ferrets. Risk telling crew they've been scooping dookie twelve hours a day for nothing. Captain calls officers into conference.

Problem: as they debate, scanners light up red with hordes of killbugs advancing on the human encampment from all sides. Captain orders to open fire. Despite the bombardment, killbug red continues to advance. The Hickey's *guns do not fall quiet until the red splotch stops squirming. Human casualties: catastrophic.*

What we don't like: lamentable state of human remains make cause of death difficult to determine, but no evidence of killbug injury among the dead. Buildings show no sign of spore damage, new or old. Every human casualty from friendly fire.

Assessment: against all reason, encampment held out for eleven months amid overwhelming enemy presence. According to logs, unit made daily assaults against primary target, the mantis factory under hill to the northwest, until the death of field commander a few weeks prior.

Question: how was it that only as the Hickey *arrived were they finally overrun?*

A lone survivor among the ruin. Pvt. Timothy Archon, recovered beyond the south palisade. At time of attack, minimally armed, appears to have been picking mushrooms. Pinned by chassis of atomic shoveler thrown by explosion. Tibia and fibula of right leg splintered, muscle tissue in tatters to mid-thigh. Doc Tir says nothing we can't regrow. Minimal limp to follow physical therapy. Not insignificant: blow to the head, moderate-to-severe concussion.

Two weeks later: combination of physical and psychological trauma has left Pvt. Archon in near constant meltdown. Shouts constantly while awake, calls out to late comrades by name, curses the earth that bore them, and praises their swimming. *Unable to rest unless sedated. Doc Tir wants to keep him under until the nanos can reduce the severity of his injury, but captain forbids it. Reason: Pvt. Archon claims to have murdered the men himself—the entire task force, ones killed by recent bombardment, plus all previous deaths, some individually, others* en masse. *Seeking to avoid a black mark on his record for annihilating all men on rock save one, captain encourages Pvt. Archon to speak, despite the distress it causes him.*

As a rule, all information provided by men claiming to be possessed by insects: suspect.

Asked if he hears voices in his head, patient insists he feels listeners *in his blood. Alien "presence" appears intermittent: Pvt. Archon goes from demanding privacy while completely alone, to complaining of abandonment while surrounded by medical personnel.*

Worthy of note: discussion of "possession" frequently accompanied by requests for certain dietary supplements. During rare calms, has no difficulty ingesting or digesting hospital food. Otherwise, fare deemed "inadequate," though ought to seem damn near gourmet after a year of K-rations. Patient pushes tray to the floor, shouting "The wrong proteins!" or "I can't synthesize this!" Demands bug-world nutriment, his mushrooms in particular, but also other plants and "gunks" from the surface. Camp logs suggest men on This One terrified of local vegetation, to eat or even touch. Data logs' only mention of ingredients for which Pvt. Archon asks in connection with a topical cream one Pvt. Grayson concocted for unstated purpose.

Pvt. Archon claims to be only remaining supporter of task force's original mission. Prior to our arrival, breakdown in military order following death of commander. The Hickey *found munitions depleted, food stores scant, fresh water supply pitiful, generator producing only coughs and wheezes of power. In light of which, task force's commitment to mission damn nigh superhuman. Yet Archon remains wrathful, calling dead men mutineers.*

During lucid moments, patient manifests no memory of statements made during delirium. Doc Tir, implementing several stratagems, has been unable to trick him into betraying any cross-awareness. The two aspects of his personality do not appear to communicate.

In claiming to be secretly responsible for death of every man on This One, patient also raves that some men suspected his bug-allied activity. I transcribe one of the less muddled diatribes below.

Cheever was too drunk to realize what his brain already knew. The answer was all over his computer screen. He was staring right at it, tearing his hair out. The scrolling numbers painted such a fat red arrow at what was going on, he ought to have understood it even brain-hammered. But his emotions and his intellect never agreed on anything. So, he calls me into his computer lab, begging me either to alleviate his fear or confirm his calculations.

"These *bwasted* twiangulation data," he cries, "do you know what they say? This V.I.B.—the *Consawt*—he's *here!* He's got to be! Sometimes the static distortion is so powerful, the bugs can barely walk. But later, nothing, it's gone. Not just moved off world, *gone* like it never existed. But the *west* of the time . . ." Suddenly the numbers on his monitor flicker and change. He screams, then laughs nervously at me. *"It's in the camp,"* he whispers. "At night, the data say *in the bawacks*, the bunks even! Yours, as far as I can tell. Are you the Consawt, Archon? Are you a goddamned kewbug? But only sometimes? Of *cawse* not. Please tell the mathematics not to *pway pwanks* on me. Tell them they are above this nonsense. Tell them!" He breaks down into drunken sobbing.

I think to myself, Cheever doesn't trust his own instincts. That protects us for now, but it'll change. We gotta take out those brains. Man! I like him, but all this high-level mathing can't continue. It's only a matter of time before his brains talk some sense into his mushy bits.

So, I put a call in.

"Yes, One?" they say.

"Look," I say, "Cheever is a good egg, but . . . Mebbe you wanna scramble his math crunchers? Just the gray stuff, okay? Is that possible? It's half gone with bwain damage already, maybe you can just give his smarts a push?"

"Yes, of course, One, we understand you. Hail, One!"

But they don't. They don't get it. Good eggs . . . you think that's funny? But of course not, their language is without nuance and they've no sense of humor at all. Cheever's head is all good eggs now.

Pvt. Archon producing killbug amino acids in urine. Presence generally precedes the onset of mutations that sometimes result from injuries due to killbug contact. Several insectoid compounds have mutagenic effect on human tissue, but blood contamination generally required before body starts developing bug organs. Pvt. Archon's medical records make no mention of so much as a scratch from bugs on This One, despite daily combat activity. Odd, since treated almost weekly for injuries incurred in and around camp, suggesting especially clumsy nature.

As said, all wounds incurred upon our arrival due to friendly fire: burns, blunt force trauma, metal splinters. Best guess: Hickey's bombardment scattered such a dense cloud of bug bits that Pvt. Archon's broken and bleeding body caught airborne contagion. In any case, patient still manifests none of the customary growths: budding feelers, compound eyes, etc.

Patient's mental profile also does not demonstrate psychoses that typically accompany insectoid mutation: psychosomatic paralysis, sensation of something devouring the flesh, aural hallucination of threatening and/or taunting voices. On the contrary, delusions of grandeur. Conjecture: prolonged danger, isolation, and exposure on This One have induced fantasy of ordering killbugs to murder comrades. Perhaps a different lone survivor would have suffered from similar self-deception.

Gil knew. No suspicions. Oh, Cheever mathed it over and had his doubts, but Gilbert Rasher kne-eeew. Coulda marched up to the Major and laid it out in language a sergeant could understand. Instead, he found it the damn funniest thing ever. Well, him'n the killbugs—listen, Tick, they're cut from the same cloth. But his head got big, see? "I will never diiiie," exclaims that shitpile. Spilling the whole damn conspiracy at mess, like it's a big joke! Winking, always winking, like it was *him*, like *he* was the Consort. Figures I won't mash him. Why? 'Cause I killed him once, and once he killed me. For Rasher, that's tighter'n family. "I'm his faaaavorite!" he says. Like if he repeats it enough, that makes it true. Anyone else pulls that shit, Gil knows I call a skyrifer down on him. But he thinks he's like a court jester with special dispensation! He keeps telling me he's my favorite so he can open his smart mouth any way he likes. And I let him do it too, 'cause what else am I gonna do?

But soon he's taking shots at me. Not smartass remarks, I mean actual bullets! Showing everybody how I can't be killed. "Oops, I shot a scorpadoo," he says. Yeah, he had the targeter zeroed on my fucking face! The bug comes rushing out of nowhere to absorb the fire. Gil acts like he can't believe his luck. *His* luck. "They just keep faaaalling in the way!" he cries. "Those dumb shits." He knows, though, he knows it's *me* who can never die, but he wants make a spectacle of it!

Think of my situation. This thing they put in my blood, made of bug boogers and what else: to them it makes me like a god. Which means I always know if there's something they don't like! Pro tip: killbugs don't care for shenanigans.

Fortunately, they're a bit soft on Gil, otherwise they'd have smeared him ages ago. But now they're giving me *the patience*, which . . . The patience is not quite a request but you are expected to fulfill it. But patience was not what *I* had, I wanted to cut his god-spiting heart out myself.

"Don't just kill him," I said, "cook that arrogant prick. Have a picnic, invite your friends, uncork a vintage." Well, it broke Gil's heart. While he was getting aerated, I stared him down, like here's a gift from me. Oh, the eyes he made. "Weren't we a team?" he seemed to say. "I set 'em up, you knock 'em down? This Consort business was our thing. It was beautiful."

Well, what can I say, Gil, you're out. See ya in hell.

Pvt. Rasher far and away the favorite subject of Pvt. Archon's delirium. He continues here:

Hell, Gil *liked* the killbugs. Sure, he'd torture and kill 'em for fun, but it rubbed him wrong to do it under orders. *For the Alliance*, the greater good and shit, all that upset his mojo. So, he had to have secondary occupations.

For instance, pouring poison in my ear.

That sad sack, Kittredge Hemlock, never wanted anything except to close his eyes and enjoy his nightmares, to watch every wonder in the galaxy conflate into a single sky-towering chimera, its diverse heads seething among the clouds.

One day Gil clears his throat. "That man," he says, "is the biggest threat to our existence. He can't wait until the encampment is destroyed. No sloop runs, no shit shovels, just living in the wilderness like he did on all those other rocks, studying his leaves and beasties until his heart's content. We're nothing but an impediment to him. Once we're gone, he's back in paradise."

"You're out of your skull," I say.

"Watch and see. He'll find a way."

Soon after, Hemlock's dragging a thorbeetle into the square. "I'm going to tinker with its fission reactor," he says. Gil stands like a shadow behind me, his posture a silent I-told-you-so.

"Bah," I say. "That bug poses no threat to anyone but Pimply Kitt himself, and he's handled monsters of every size on every rock in the galaxy. Plus, he has an advanced degree in bio-atomic energy, he knows what he's doing."

Gil smiles wryly. "Exactly," he says. "Imagine you're

Kitt, dreaming of how you could be free of all this. The only question is, how long till you find the guts to make it happen? Imagine if a massive power surge from this Thorbeetle fried all our equipment: that'd be the end of us. But Hemlock would survive. He'd hide up a tree, in a cave, or under a pile of shit. And he'd be happier that way. It's a mistake to trust him."

All this preyed on my own silent wishes. It was *me*, not Kitt, who'd think no action too vile to make this ugly war disappear, to return to the carefree melancholy of my youth. But I didn't believe I could even contemplate such things. Naturally, when Gil attributed them to Kitt, I believed him.

I wonder sometimes if the bugs didn't recruit Rasher to wear down my reluctance to giving kill orders. One shamefully unnecessary death and I'd belong to them. After Hemlock, there was no turning back. In retrospect, it should've been Gilbert I had killed—first and only! By the time I worked my way down to him, it'd have been just as well to let him stick around. At least then I wouldn't have felt so alone.

Barring fantastic coincidence, the camp being overrun upon the hour of our arrival requires explanation. Some of Hickey's *command team suggest the killbugs, having gained intelligence of our arrival, desired to trick us into destroying our men, even at the cost of own combatants. Unclear what objective this would serve, but consistent with other killbug tactics which place little value on troop survival. Others propose that killbugs, having deemed the human presence to be no threat, were observing task force's operations in a scientific manner. Our sudden return compelled them to make formal conclusion to the study.*

Although advanced strategic intelligence of this sort might exonerate the captain of wrongdoing, he prefers to believe killbugs are brutes incapable of critical thought. He has therefore ordered medical staff to entertain the possibility that the bugs were enticed into the camp by Pvt. Archon, as he himself suggests.

Ordering killbugs to attack by means of secret dreams, however, amounts to black magic. Doc Tir argues that, if issuing commands in such a way were possible, the method would involve the subsonic signals killbugs use to communicate through space. However, this organic process is poorly understood. Here in killbug territory, space is so saturated with these distortions, it can't be determined whether any such signals originate with Pvt. Archon.

The subsonic transmitter is usually an organ the size of a fist, but varies from species to species. Perhaps for the honorific role Pvt. Archon claims to possess—various names include

Consort, Death-namer, One, and Opifex Avatar—the bugs have bio-engineered a microscopic organette to elude medical detection. Bio-scans have located no such thing in his physiology. Possible the micro-transmitter has left his body: bug protein no longer appears in his urine.

Must be said: examinations of Pvt. Archon have been perfunctory, as the ferret concern now occupies most of medical technicians' time. Doc Tir is forced to devote a growing portion of energy to injuries incurred by crew during legging matches. Unclear why in subspace polecats refuse to cage-fight but turn savage when stuffed down some poor bastard's trousers. Wounds inflicted on crew frequently require delicate reconstructive surgery. Captain has issued ban on ferret legging, but as Cmdr. Griff says, Hickey's life support already over-strained, a little natural selection might be called for.

Besides, if ferrets have been seized in accordance with an Alliance housing regulation, rightfully they are property of the fleet. Shipmen have the captain over a barrel if he wishes them to keep quiet about his private acquisition of prohibited fauna, so it pays to be lenient, especially when it's their own nuts on the line.

Not only captains must be indulgent. Gods too. Pvt. Archon explains.

"Excuse the Hive, One," they say. "We're happy to be slaughtered, yes. Of course we are, in obedience to you, in the name of the Greater Death. We serve you, you serve the Hive. Hail the Hive! But Boogo, sir, that one's a warrior. A cyclone. We are willing to endure Boogo today and Boogo tomorrow, but honor the Hive's sacrifice, One. Show us you're on the team, give us Boogo. Bear any burden, that's us, but it's been six months now. Give him as a token of faith. Listen. It is not for us, the commanders, that we ask. *We* understand, we'll absorb causalities all year, every day for a millennium if we have to, gladly. But some of our guys got neural nodes the size of peas. Really, sir, peas! They're not afraid to die, but they feel it's unbuggy to endure a smearing patiently. So give them Boogo. Show 'em you're on their side."

Well, what choice do I have? I put the mark on Oogs.

"But make it look good," I say, "he's our Achilles, he goes out like a hero! Large and in charge. That's all he wants anyway, to die with bug meat in his face. So give it to him. Let him tear some new asses, one last time, hear?"

Like kids on Christmas. "Of course, One, of course! Hail hail. You're the best."

Even if fanciful, the details of Pvt. Archon's delusions are usually meticulously rendered. At certain moments, however, they deteriorate into a brand of nonsense so mischievous, it's as if he's taunting us. Consider the following:

Little Dungmeata couldn't keep her ass closed. Suddenly Grayson was divulging high-level killbug secrets in his pain-wracked delirium: fuckhill schematics, factory procedures, like he's one of the family.

"We make pillow talk," she says to me, "harmless."

"Really," I say, "is that all? Because it's not enough for a mantis mother to be a killbug in war, she needs to be a killbug *in bed.* Which means, you should be the one gathering intelligence from *him.*"

My agent is bemused. "You want me to report back your own side's secrets to you?"

I sigh. "Yes! I need to test the line's integrity, Dungmeata. I must be sure Grayson is willing to betray humanity, otherwise I can't use him. So, I need access to the information he's feeding you, so I can tell if it is up to snuff."

"Right," she says. "I should shut up and listen."

"No!" I cry. "Silence is lethal. The key is how to say the right things."

She nods. "Lie to him. Yes, boss, understood."

So innocent, she.

"Incorrect," I say. "Tell the truth. And not merely the

material truth, the *essential* truth. Because hominid intelligence expects anything that comes through your channels to be contaminated, so you need to load the pipe with as much verifiable intelligence as possible. The more they confirm, the less they'll trust whatever else you say."

Dungmeata shifts uncomfortably. "Listen," she says, "you know I'm your agent either way. It'd help if I knew which side am I working for when I'm talking to you."

I smile condescendingly at the pretty fool. "Darling Dungmeata," I say, "intelligence, counterintelligence, it's a complex game. You gotta spill beans to get beans. Every few years the bean counters assess who's *bean* up and you find out who's winning the espionage game. Meanwhile, everyone's in bed with everyone else. Often literally. It's a clusterfuck. But we must be careful lest somebody gets confused and starts playing by the rules. Because then they have to be eliminated."

"By whom," she asks.

"Doesn't matter," I say. "Our side, their side—who knows which is which anyway? But the moment an agent comprehends his own function, somebody has to smear 'em."

I study Dungmeata's face. She's drooling. Nothing

unusual. She drools constantly. Still, I make careful note of it.

"Why are you telling me this?" she asks.

I act frustrated because this is a reasonable question. "Listen, here's what you need to know about espionage. Many agents do nothing but leak information to the enemy. Yet they still consider themselves patriots. Why? Because serving the wrong side is *their job*. The first thing they teach you in spy school is to eradicate your fundamental loyalties. Loyalty limits the flow of info out, which limits the flow of info in. Which for a spy is basically treason."

"But if I report to you and I don't know what side you're on, how do I know which is the wrong side?"

"Oh bollygop," I say, frowning. "This is very bad news. I'm afraid you've just compromised yourself, Dungmeata. I'm afraid this means death. You'll have to eliminate Grayson."

The drool splatters in a puddle at her feet. "What does Grayson have to do with what I just said?" she asks.

"Nothing," I say sadly. "And he will pay for it with his life."

"I don't understand this conversation at all," she replies.

"Oh, I think you understand a little *too* well, Secret Agent Dungmeat, Feminine Diminutive!"

But in the end, the joke was on me. Turns out the intel I got from Grayson was only what that bitch Little Dungmeata mumbled after Grayson loaded her full of hallucinogens and convinced her he was her mother. A little fact checking, though, quickly revealed most of the information he mined from Dungmeata was incorrect, meaning either Dungmeata was cognizant enough to provide counterintelligence even in her altered state, or Grayson was deliberately contaminating the information he collected. Probably both.

Which, if you've been in this business as long as I have, means Dungmeata was counterfeiting her ignorance of espionage to conceal how both she and Grayson belonged to an underground killbug plot sworn to neutralize the Consort, one of them a legitimate member and the other a mole, although neither knew which was which. By following my directive to eliminate Grayson, Dungmeata recognized she was destroying evidence of her affiliation in case she ever found herself on her own trail. Therefore, it had been me who had been *her* agent all along!

Listen, Tick. You might believe the purpose of intelligence and espionage is to discover or conceal the truth, but it's quite the opposite: it's to give the impression that the truth is buried somewhere under all that confusion, however helplessly. Espionage is the business of creating the *illusion of causality*, and more importantly, the semblance of control. Money gets transferred from bank account to bank account, data is downloaded from computer to computer, then, unfortunately, somebody dies. Something is *happening*, yes? Only in a technical sense. But as long as *something happens*, the galaxy is safe for now. Unless it isn't. Understand? Excellent.

By the way, Tick, these are all lies I'm making up to confuse you. Except for the parts that are true.

Pvt. Archon addresses me as Tick in a teasing, perhaps affectionate vein. He appropriated the name from Doc Tir, who, always pressed for time, punctuates all his instructions with his impression of an analog clock.

The patient's restriction from painkillers and sedatives has made his temperament unpleasant. To lighten his mood, the shipmen sometimes bring him to the hangar to watch the legging matches, spotting him funds to place a wager or two. He glowers at the proceedings with smug contempt, expressing disapproval of both ferrets and trouser-wearers. "Mammals," he mutters under his breath. The affectation is so absurd, it's hard to imagine it is not conceit.

Most but not all species in the Hominid Infantry are mammals. Turns out, some aren't even hominids.

Clarker was part of a military experiment to genetically modify canines to serve as combat troops. Since dogs mature quickly, it ought to have been feasible to cultivate them for the front faster than humans. (This proves they were planning a generational war from the start.) The loyalty and ferocity of a dog, the cunning of a man—that was the idea. What a disaster. Coprophagia of a dog, humping agility of a man. Weapon handling of a dog. Adaptive thinking of a dog, hygiene of a dog, stomach-turning facial features of a freakish man-dog hybrid. Looked and moved like an ape wearing a dead man's skin as a costume.

Imagine any dog you know doing everything he does with people parts. You are picturing Clarker. What a horror.

I say to him, "Joe, you can't act like that anymore, you're a person now. They stuck tubes in your ass and altered your DNA, so it's no longer acceptable to thrust your head in my crotch just 'cause you feel lonely."

He smiles his stupid hound grin in reply. "You slell like

shit!" he yelps liplessly. He means it as a compliment. Shit was everywhere, but somehow it smelled better between my legs than anywhere else. Fucking mutt.

As kids on Beta, when we chose sides for the frolic, Clarker and I were the last two picked, always. The captains stroked their chins for twenty minutes before deciding between us: "Hmm, Archon or Clarker, Clarker or Archon, hm-mmm. Should we pick the dumb drooling animal who'll probably drown us, or should we pick Joe Clarker?" Ha, ha, good one! The same joke as yesterday, but still fresh and funny. "Dumb drooling animal." Ha ha ha!

Those louts really couldn't tell brains from frolic. If you didn't appreciate their stupid sport, they assumed you couldn't dress yourself either. Idiots. I was better frolicker than half of them anyways. They just didn't like me, and they used Joe to make it clear.

When the bugs ashed the Earth, I enlisted at gunpoint like everyone else. I thought, well, at least now I'm free of that hellbeast. Then the military's Operation Doggy Doo happened. Ten years I've fought this war, Tick. Ten years, you think a dog would get old and die. Life extension was the only part of the genetic modification they got right. Fuck hell, why waste resources working out that part? Those freaks were just spore fodder anyway, no different than us. But nothing could touch a hair on Clarker without touching Oogo first. And Oogo was immortal . . . until he wasn't. Fucking mutt nearly lived forever.

To be honest, I wrote Clarker's eulogy in a spiteful mood. I hoped it'd be the most bitterly ironic speech anyone had ever heard. About how in the darkness of space he'd been a glowing beacon of humanity. The men just ate it up. They laughed, they cheered, they cried. Because nothing is more absurd now than human dignity. What's even the point of having thoughts or feelings if the galaxy is filled with people like that? Fight and die all you like, whom are you doing it for? I was so disgusted I nearly walked off the podium in the middle of it.

They really had no memory of the humiliation they put me through with that mutt. Over years as hard as the ones we've been through, I guess a lot of the old ill-feelings get buried over. Well, that day, they all broke the surface again. For me, anyway. Nothing I said reminded them of the shitty things they once did. Of what dumb drooling animals they were.

Ferret meat is delicious. Not as versatile as space pork, but more tender and we don't have to eat it salted. Preservation of ferrets has been made possible by the demise of the task force on This One, which has aroused feelings of guilt toward the perished men and bloodthirstiness toward the ferrets themselves. A reckoning has begun for our furry friends. Several have been found poisoned or mutilated inside their terraria.

So, you can't even cook them. What a waste.

Pvt. Archon's miraculous survival has also earned him the suspicions of the crew. Due to abrasive temperament, not even his injuries or psychological trauma win him sympathy. He glares at his caretakers in a way that makes them feel like spiders dangling over the flame. The little scissor gesture he makes with his fingers insinuates they haven't much time.

Yet when his fever breaks, the patient is disturbingly docile. If you raise your voice, he becomes timid, quick to comply with any request you make of him. However, rather than softening the crew's opinion of him, this double nature makes them even more distrustful.

It doesn't help he takes pride in telling lies. Consider:

Everything I'll ever do or say is eclipsed by Roger Kean's shadow. Fact. When I spoke at his funeral, I claimed I altered his journal so we would be remembered more favorably in his posthumously published writing. Nobody believed I did that. The moving speech I quoted him giving, no one suspected I wrote that too. Roger Kean uttered so many soul-stirring flights of eloquence in his life, who could remember them all? And it sounded like him. No one will ever acknowledge it could be a forgery. But that's not my concern.

I wanted to prove I could give the galaxy a Roger Keaning as good as anybody. I wrote some speeches, composing them in my head to pass the time while I shoveled shit. Just to see if they'd go over, I stuffed one in that hideous asscrack Roger Kean called a mouth. Hey, remember this fake speech, I asked? Sure, they all said. Their exhausted, electroshocked brains would remember anything I told them to.

All that talk of duty and redemption—what a heap of noise you are, Roger Kean!

The truth is, I liked to hear him speak, I liked the sound of those round, archaic Kean family vowels. But those golden words with which he slathered the men, they never stuck to us.

Similarly, Roger Kean was covered in a magic oil that made every ugly thing slide right off him. While we all took a saucing in the sloops, never a single clump of shit stuck to his hair. If there was a power struggle, it didn't matter if he got trounced, publicly he'd come off the victor. His worst enemies admired him and craved his friendship, knowing their image would be improved by his proximity.

He even had the good fortune to die at the right moment, just after his star had peaked but still seemed on the rise.

He was born with all that good taint on him, and we buried it with him.

But the Roger Kean for the ages, I realized I could make myself part of that. If he would only die—say, right around now—it'd leave me three months for file hacking and rewriting. I could become history's voice of Roger Kean, borrowing a few lines from his video diaries to lend credence. Then when posterity warmed itself by Roger Kean's immortal flame, it'd be *me* making their asses toasty. After they make an Alamo out of this debacle. After—let's face it—*I've* made it an Alamo. Nobody will know the truth. And that's fine. The knowledge that I pissed in the pool of history is enough for me.

Discovery this had been the Roger Kean mission: disaster. Some relief we didn't kill him ourselves, but fate of Kean's task force will attract attention across the Alliance. Captain now sees our problem as threefold.

One: our bombardment might suggest a conspiracy to eliminate Kean in the unlikely case of his survival. The low hanging fruit in the emergent blame game: us.

Two: danger of antagonizing anyone bold enough to murder

a son of an Interworld Military Council Member. If Pvt. Archon is agent of some assassination plot, bringing him back to the fleet alive might make whoever gave him orders agitated enough to exact reprisals on captain and crew.

Three: Even the most cursory investigation of this matter likely to uncover myriads of illegal ferrets.

On less pressing note: salvage technicians have located and examined Kean's personal log. Damaged in the bombing, some lacunae appear, but all entries stamped with atomic dating and sealed shortly after his death. The colorful embellishments which Archon claims to have made during his funeral speech do not appear. No reason to doubt content in Kean's journal is genuine.

"Don't touch Peter." That was my explicit instruction. "You already devoured everything innocent in him. Somehow, it's left him no worse than he was. So, I demand you to leave what's left, leave him his life. You wanted Boogo? Fine. Now spare me Peter Anglewood."

I could almost hear them nibbling their lips. "We're here to kill, One, not to protect."

Silence. Waiting for me to concede what I could not.

"But the choice of you as Death-namer pleases the Hive; anybody else, we'd do this gratefully. But Anglewood, One? He may not be within our power."

The answer devastated me. I had already known nothing in the galaxy could save a man like that. Not during a time like this.

I admired Peter's intense faith, the childlike joy with which he envisioned of the future. *The extinguishment of the galaxy, hooray!*

In singing of horrors, he betrayed how he alone was immune to the horror around him. No matter how desperate the situation, the future always survived in his imagination in a way it never survived in mine. Not a sterile, lead-brick Roger Kean tomorrow, but one where, each summer, everyone reunites for a picnic at the municipal gorge—family, friends, new arrivals from the Old World, aged parents, lost cousins, talc-powdered tottering snot-piles born on the Betan moons—a future where we relive the past and spread gossip, eat ice cream and those little sausages you just can't get anymore. For Peter, *that* was real life. The war was just an illusion. One day this would all be over and he'd go back to watching his little cousins skin their knees as they race along the Shepridge rock fissures.

He never fully understood of what death orgies and the destruction of the galaxy meant, not really. He was like a religious zealot enthusiastic about the Second Coming without giving a damn what it is. Time and again, in the sloops or beyond the palisade, he threw himself in the maw of some inexorable thing, secure in his faith in the future. When by miracle he survived, it only gave him the courage to do it again. You can't save someone like that, no matter how much you beg or bribe.

Peter Anglewood dressed for war like a children's party, ready to get himself killed every day, twice a day. Death would have taught him nothing. Eventually, the peedlebugs ate him out of embarrassment. The travesty just needed to end. His antics had made even death a charade.

That he was a poet, I could forgive him. What is a poet? Someone who lets you down repeatedly, someone you can count on to disappoint you—yet you still believe in them. A poet: the best they can do is pretty bad, but you want them in there when everything's on the line. You choke down embarrassment while you cheer them on. "Hey, watch this guy make a jackass out of us and everything we strive for." Poet.

Look, I'll call poet anything except someone who makes poetry, anything but that. Because I want—I *need* poetry to be out there, I just don't want to endure it.

Once for giggles, I said to Anglewood, "Hey, let's have

a poem." He got as far as one word—a gerund. I said "Nope." Nothing you ever want to hear begins with a gerund. "Stop!" I cried. I fell to the ground, clutching my side in agony. "Truly, Anglewood, you are a Smasher of Worlds! Go, make poetry until you've destroyed us all. God speed, but over there. Also: shut up."

He smiled and bowed, stretching his fluttering hand down to the ankle.

That's the future right there.

The nanobots have completed the first phase of reconstruction on Pvt. Archon's lower body. Although painful rehabilitation still awaits him, he is through the worst of it, and his discomfort has become more manageable. Continues to speak copiously and feverishly about men and their fates, but more fantastic elements have begun to vanish. Frantic gesticulation of earlier raving replaced with more static rumination.

The following is an amalgam of several discourses.

The men resented me because I'm from an exporter family. None of us ever had rag dust staining our nails or suffered any of the back curvature, the bone chips, or the overdeveloped shoulders. My parents were grandchildren of colonists, with all the insecurity that entails. They came as refugees from Earth, fleeing poverty or the law or ostracism—who could even say anymore?—dregs of the galaxy hellbent on not repeating our ancestors' mistakes.

We arrived in the Beta system with no place left to stake our claim except a wretched patch in the mountains on the ugliest of the outer moons. The fourth! It was a blasted country, nothing but dust and glittery rocks. When those rocks turned out to be worth more than gold, damned right we made them pay through the nose. We hadn't crossed the galaxy to be spat on *here*. Instead of digging the ore ourselves, we paid bent shadows to cart it away for us. And not much either: the sudden shift in climate to electrical storms had ravaged the economy. The pittance wage we offered was a charity.

Soon a political movement pushed for the restoration of all ragnarite mines to public ownership. Here we saw an opportunity. "Let Beta's natural resources belong to the miners!" we cried. Heroic, us. The ore's real value was on the interworld market anyway. We surrendered our claims in exchange for exclusive rights to ship ragnarite off Beta for the next twenty years. Ragnarite is extremely volatile in space, but we developed a technique to transport it safely, and we formed a Consortium to protect our monopoly on interstellar shipping.

With our trade secret secure, we practically dared any

upstart Betan competitors to bankrupt themselves delivering dust. Offworld engineers developed their own method, but conditions in the mines were brutal and laborers were always ready to strike. The Consortium offered to quell any disquiet on Beta if the government of Earth kept foreign ships out of our ports. The Kean family negotiated the treaty for us, that's how they won their power and reputation.

From then on, we clung to a tenuous prosperity founded on dumb luck, relying on ruthlessness, and under attack from all directions: local taxation, interworld tariffs, labor unions, plagues among the workers, other exporters trying to muscle us out of our share of the operation. And the inheritance rights of too many descendants.

Let's put it this way: after three generations, my family had no skills except making other people's stuff look like their stuff. When I wasn't playing with my toys, my brother William went around showing them to everyone until anyone would say they were *his* toys. As he got older, he learned to do this with anything: a place at the table, a cave speeder, a girlfriend. Squatting was the family enterprise, and he was a natural. So, to whom should control of the family business fall? I had the brains, but he was the clever one. Even I admit this.

With the destruction of Earth, the galaxy's glutton for ragnarite, our commercial interests fell into doubt. William was chosen to sniff out future markets and warm them with his ass until no one could contest the Archons' share of the enterprise. But military service would be needed to legitimize the family's stakes. So, while William oversaw the rebranding of ragnarite, Timothy would shoot the bugs. Fighting shoulder-to-shoulder with the rag men would smooth over the Archons' public relations game enormously. If Timothy got himself killed, all the better.

But sons of rag farmers are not moved by loss of privilege. Was I supposed to tell them they mustn't shun me, I was in the same boat as them now, even if my father's spine wasn't ruined the way theirs was? They only remembered my family used them badly, they didn't care the rest of the Alliance had used them even worse, that those ragwhores from Earth used to wonder aloud if Betan bluebacks were even human.

I can't stand to touch them. Even to look at them makes me queasy. They sense it, it makes them indignant, why shouldn't it? But digging filth makes you filthy. All things equal, what is not filthy is better than what is. Accidents of birth don't change that.

The rag farmers have a culture of insults, like all trash

do. If you want to be one of them, you gotta know how to dish it and how to eat it. It's called ragging, right? That's how they recognize their own. But if *I* insult them, it's Consortium putting them down, it's insult to injury. If I don't want to get knifed, I have to be polite: praise their heroes, defame their enemies. This costs me their respect. Also, it's tricky, because whom they like and whom they don't is fluid and guarded from me. Sometimes I pick up clues: if they talk too well of someone, they hate him, that's for sure, he's a half inch from getting it in the neck. If they abuse a man in public, they might be willing to lay their lives down for him, but only maybe, you must be careful.

The plus side is: being who I once was, they're afraid of me in ways even they don't know about. Sometimes they almost salute me, forgetting they don't have to. Sometimes I catch them refusing to salute, betraying the deference they feel they owe.

Whoever stands over the dead exerts a kind of ownership over life, that's true everywhere. They shouldn't have let me do it, be the eulogizer. That's why I stole the privilege and made them think they forced me into it. 'Cause for them it's a special conundrum: to eulogize they have to say something nice, but to say something nice is kind of a defamation coming from another rag man. Besides, those brutes would barely know how.

So, among them, they've got a little sub-caste: shit-ons with special permission to say nice things when nice things need to be said, like at funerals. Filth, even by their standards. You'd never envy them, but they get a place of honor on these occasions, and the rest of the time they are taken care of materially—food and a place to live—and nobody is allowed to hurt them.

This is the role I co-opted. No one wanted to give the eulogies, so I say like I'm talking to myself, "Well, I'd certainly never do it." So, they say, "How about we have Tim do it? If he does it right, swell. If he doesn't, we have an excuse, yeah?"

Tim does it.

In the speech, Tim puts himself down a little. He also speaks a bit ill of the dead so it's got some Betan flavor. Now they feel comfortable. Suddenly he's valuable. They don't like him or trust him, but they protect him.

Harvey Croop was even more an outsider among the men than the Archons. At least my family was integral to their way of life. As an opponent of ragnarite, Croop stood openly against their entire worldview. Without his cunning, courage, and patience, the men knew they were lost, that's true. But the reason he could lead them was because they would never have taken orders from one of their own, they had to be ruled by a foreign prince. The Major vowed to share their fate, so they anointed him with oil.

But it got under my skin how he actually loved those men, believed in them, as if they were capable of feeling anything beyond anger and petty jealousy. How did he find a way to accept them for who they were, yet always push them further? Isn't that a contradiction?

Well, I was convinced it wasn't magic. In a vacuum of power, they'd follow someone else. Men don't obey a leader out of love or even fear, but because they need someone to mediate the jealousies between themselves. They scarcely care what you cheat them out of, what humiliations you put them through, so long as they think they'll make out better than their neighbors.

After Croop died, overwhelming enemy presence still loomed on three sides. They needed someone to hold them together, to save them from anarchy. Here was my chance, I thought, to cement my place among them. Invoking Croop's name, I called them to me. I hurled brilliant oratory that could have moved a stone to tears. But they stared back unblinking as fish. I didn't even rouse their anger. "Sit down, Archon," they said. "Drink some bwain damage with us. The ships or death, either way, it won't be long now."

So, they waited. I brooded and festered. I realized I couldn't go back. In the infantry, you're used to everyone in each other's business, but on Thisone there was a special intimacy: bigger, more profound. No one needs to know what we did to survive those eleven months. I've told you things, but I haven't told you anything. I knew these men by touch, smell, and taste, like they knew me. If you think I'm saying something sexual, that's not even the start of it. Each man became a part of the other until we were a single twisted organism. We wiped a collective asshole, we had no secrets.

That's why the prospect of our departure constituted a crisis. Imagine you had a severed arm living off somewhere apart from you. You might prefer it had died. Anyway, that's how I felt. I didn't want the secrets of that place surviving beyond my reach. Let a mantle of silence descend over it all, I thought. Someday an outsider would ask questions and someone among them might speak, telling secrets rightfully carried to our graves. Well, I fixed that. Now the grave is where they are.

All of them.

Captain has decided what's done is done, no helping the dead. Shall issue the following report: task force unwittingly built encampment over an anti-aircraft spore silo, which Hickey *neutralized in advance of landing. With forethought, inquiry ought to be weatherable, since none likely to fly out and investigate claims.*

Remainder of ferrets saved. Cmdr. Griff has located a zoo on Tiptoogan willing to fence them for us, on pretense of having been breeding them for generations. Hickey's *maintenance log to be doctored to make detour to Tiptoogan appear necessary. Crew informed price per head shall be only twenty percent of estimated market value. An outrage, but in volume ferrets should still turn a tidy sum. Suspicion: officers will skim before dividing spoils. Crew furious but will do nothing.*

Arrangements made for Pvt. Archon to disappear: scheduled to travel by supply ship to medical asteroid in remote Fenrir system where mutant cases are researched outside the theater of conflict. Mutations are generally fatal; this facility handles rare patients who do not expire despite physical transformation. Goal to study how these outliers manage infection in hope of developing treatment or immunization. Appearance of bug protein in Pvt. Archon's urine sufficient to qualify him as a patient. Perhaps mystery of his survival will be unraveled too.

Asteroid receives supply ships only every few years. Convenient for us: by time Archon returns to fleet, state of war likely to have changed so drastically, for good or ill, this incident no longer of interest to anyone.

Starboat Dennis Hickey's *next mission: respond to distressed science vessel near Sugarhose Nebula. Maps place it in contested space, but sensors report only intermittent comet-tooth activity over last six months. Should be possible to shuttle in a repair crew without entanglements.*

The Hickey *will not communicate back with the fleet until our return from the nebula, so I am blackboxing this report in case of incident. Pvt. Archon's unlikely claims have me a little spooked, but I've convinced myself if I'm overcautious, nothing will come of it. I've appended transcripts of Pvt. Archon's funeral oratory, either for documentation of the patient's psychological profile or a description of the killbugs' cosmogony, whichever is deemed more useful. I suspect whoever finds this record among the wreck of the* Hickey *will be more interested in the ferret trade than the This One mission, but I know firsthand that deep space salvage is a tedious occupation. I hope perusing these documents has proved at least more entertaining than getting your genitals noshed by a frightened weasel.*

ABOUT THE AUTHOR

Will Madden is a Nashville based author, originally from the Bronx, New York. He holds a degree in something ridiculous from a fancy institution of higher education. By day he performs menial labor so that by night he has enough brain power to deliver the hard-hitting truths about the struggles of imaginary monsters. He juggles and knits.

THANKS FOR READING!

Feel free to contact the author at silverstrigil.net and share your experience of this book. You can also sign up for the author's newsletter for bonus material, giveaways, artwork, and information about future books.

Independent authors rely on reviews from readers, so consider leaving your thoughts on sites like Goodreads or wherever you purchase books online. It means a lot!

Printed in Great Britain
by Amazon

11598731R00171